KEEPSAKE

Dan Holt

MaxHoltMedia

CONTENTS

PROLOGUE

A Research Ship 4000 miles across, like a planet turned inside out, was dispatched to survey the Orion Spur, an arm of the Milky Way Galaxy. It picked up a fission *hot spot;* a telltale sign of a developing civilization, through its space fabric sensors. The vessel dispatched two crafts; each with an instructor and a crew of four selected from the hundreds of students assigned to the information-gathering mission.

All crewmembers were supplied with safety devices that, when activated, would generate a field that would bend light rays around the student creating a bubble of invisibility. A secondary function of the safety device was as a Locator Beacon. Upon insertion of a small sphere supplied to each student, the unit would transmit the student's location to the Research Ship, facilitating rescue. The safety devices were fitted around the waist of each student and could not be removed until they returned safely to the Research Ship. Each sphere was electronically tuned to its own safety device. Were a sphere to be separated from its unit it would automatically activate a proximity function. In the event of a mishap, the student would insert the sphere into the unit and wait for rescue.

The two shuttles that were dispatched to investigate the discovery would be loaded into a Transfer Ship, a sphere-shaped vessel 300 feet in diameter that would proceed to the Solar System and locate the planet with the telltale signature, hold at a Lagrange Point, and launch the shuttles. The launch point was located 195,505 miles from the third planet and 43,495 miles from its single moon.

The shuttles were launched but were never heard from again.

Until....

Chapter 1

BUCK ANDERSON

Roswell, New Mexico

Wednesday July 5, 1947 – 4:45 a.m.

"Formation – on the double!"

Private First Class Buck Anderson snapped awake at the sound of the Duty Sergeant's voice. Buck jumped to his feet and dressed. He quickly buffed the toes of his boots with yesterday's socks. In three minutes, he went outside to the barren ground in front of the barracks. The fourth man to exit the door he quickly assumed his spot in the squad lineup; third man from the left. A few minutes later, the entire twelve-man squad was in place.

Buck, standing at rigid attention, saw a jeep skid to a stop fifty feet away, in front of the fourth platoon, second squad. A Captain stepped out of the vehicle and hurried to the squad leader's side, spoke to him quietly, then returned to the jeep and it sped away. The squad leader faced his troops.

"Squad, you will visit the mess hall then report to the Motor Pool at 0600 – dismissed."

Buck entered the mess hall, pulled off his fatigue cap, tucked it under his belt, and advanced through the line.

"What happened?" he asked the cook as he held his tray out for toast with sausage gravy.

"I don't know," the cook replied. "The Mess Sergeant put us on duty an hour early. He didn't give us a reason." Buck finished half the food, dumped the rest in the large garbage can, set the tray on the stainless steel table, and headed for the Motor Pool. The Platoon Sergeant was waiting beside a deuce-and-a-half truck. The squad was ordered to get in the back.

The truck lunged forward, headed north through the city, then turned left on a blacktop road. They were headed west. A mile down the road Buck saw a highway sign: Hwy 48. He heard the whine of the dual wheels of the two-and-a-half-ton vehicle on the road as he watched the cactus and sagebrush pass by in the distance.

"Pine Lodge Road," he whispered to himself, "that goes by Boy Scout Mountain in the Lincoln National Forest. What happened; plane crash or something?" The truck slowed then made a left turn onto a dirt road. The driver proceeded several minutes then stopped the vehicle and engaged the front axle, powering all three axles of the heavy vehicle, then took a left turn off the road and drove cross country. Buck watched the bushes and small trees pop up behind the truck as they passed under it. Buck and his comrades were jostled around as the powerful vehicle made progress. Half an hour later, the truck stopped and the driver killed the engine. An officer appeared behind the truck, a face Buck hadn't seen before, and barked orders to the squad.

"Men, out of the truck; let's move!" The squad scrambled out of the truck, lined up in formation, and came to attention. The officer scanned the squad from side to side then spoke with the voice of authority.

"Gentlemen, where you are and what you are doing is classified. You will not talk among yourselves nor discuss it with anyone else. Is that clear?" There were random *"yes sirs"* from the squad. The officer repeated with intensity: *"Is that clear!"* The squad redressed the position of attention and shouted in unison: "Yes Sir!"

The officer stood for a moment and eyed the men and then started walking around to the front of the truck. "Follow me." Buck and the rest of the squad followed, stepping over limbs, ducking under branches, walking on the rocky uneven terrain covered in pine needles, until they topped a small hill. The officer stopped. Buck stopped and looked at the scene down the gentle slope. There was a swath cut through the trees sloping down from the north. At the end of it was a huge rock the size of an automobile, cracked in half. Leaning up on it at a forty-five-degree angle was a disc-shaped craft about twenty-five feet in diameter. It was bronze and silver in color and had a hole in the side of it about four feet wide.

An officer inside the disc was handing a small body to another officer on the ground. It looked like a midget with a swollen head and a frail body. There were three others lying on the ground on a blanket with a circle of officers standing around them. There were shiny bits of metal lying on the ground all around the disc and some lodged in the trees. A sergeant approached the squad and handed each of them a cloth bag.

"Pick up everything here that's not rocks, leaves, or pine needles." Buck took the cloth bag then looked down at the bits of shiny material then back up at the sergeant. He was walking back toward the disc. Buck and his follow soldiers began picking up the material and placing it in the cloth bags. It was a tedious job picking the small pieces out of the grass and weeds; pieces quarter-sized and smaller. Soon, Buck came to a larger piece about four by twelve inches. It was bronze colored and lodged partially in the ground. He pulled it out of the ground and worked it into the bag. A smoky black-colored sphere, the size of a golf ball, rolled up between his feet. He glanced around; everyone was busy. He picked up the sphere and paused. He felt no weight. He held it two inches from the ground and released it. It slowly floated to the ground between his boots. It appeared to be metal. He made a decision; he held the cloth bag close to his person then slipped the black ball into the bloused fold of his fatigue pants at the top of his boot.

He glanced toward the saucer. There was a sergeant leaning up against it talking to another sergeant. The little people, the blanket, and the officers, all, were gone. He quickly resumed the chore of gathering the wreckage and bagging it along with the rest of the squad.

Chapter 2

THE PROMISE

Arlington, Texas

June 15th, 1985—2:30 a.m.

Raymond and Kathleen Stevens were awakened by the incessant ringing of the bedside phone. Ray turned on the lamp and picked up the receiver. He listened for a moment, and then handed it to Kathleen. "It's your sister, Marie."

Kathleen put the phone to her ear. "Marie, what is it?" Kathleen listened for several moments then spoke into the phone. "We'll be there as soon as we can." She handed the phone back to Ray and got out of bed. Ray followed. He knew it was what they had been expecting for some time. Her father's health had been slowly deteriorating since her mother passed away two years earlier. He was sixty years old but looked and walked much older.

"We have to go to Wichita Falls right away," Kathleen said with a strain in her voice. "Dad's had a heart attack. Marie said the doctors told her to notify the family."

"I'll wake up Brandon," Ray said. "You better pack a bag." Kathleen nodded and pulled a suitcase from the closet.

Ray tapped on Brandon's door and opened it, went in, and turned on the overhead light. Brandon didn't stir. He was rolled up in the covers until only his face showed.

"Brandon, wake up," Ray said as he stepped over to his twelve-year-old son's bed. Ray grasped his shoulders and shook him gently. "Son, wake up," he repeated. Brandon moaned and opened his eyes, then looked up at his father. He cleared his throat, looked at the clock, then raised his head and stared at it. He looked at his father again and blinked the question.

"Get up and get dressed, son," Ray said. "Your grandfather's in the hospital. We have to go to Wichita Falls tonight." Ray went back to his and Kathleen's bedroom and dressed.

Brandon Lee Stevens sat up for a moment and then unwrapped himself from the bedclothes. He slipped on his pants and went to the living room just as his mother came out of the bedroom. She glanced at him.

"Finish dressing, Bandon, we'll be leaving in a few minutes."

"What happened, Mom?"

His mother stopped and walked up to Brandon and hugged him. "Your grandfather's had a heart attack and we have to go to the hospital right away."

"Is he going to be okay?"

"We don't know. You'd better pack a change of clothes." Brandon nodded and returned to his room, finished dressing, and got his clothes. When he returned to the living room, the front door was open and his father was carrying a suitcase to the car. Brandon followed him and put his bag in too. The sound of tree frogs filled the dark night. In the distance, he could hear the occasional sounds of the city. The only lighting was a streetlight a half a block away and the splash of light from the open door of the house. Brandon shivered. He went back to his room and got his jacket.

Wichita Falls, Texas

The Sun was just peeping over the horizon when they drove into the parking lot of the Wichita General Hospital. Brandon awakened with a start when the car stopped. He raised up and looked out the window at the scattered array of automobiles in the spacious parking lot, then looked toward the main building. He rubbed the side of his head where it had lain against the car door for the past two hours. He got out of the car and followed his mom and dad to the hospital Emergency Room entrance. They went inside and paused in the hall. His mother stepped over to the information desk and then returned.

"He's on the third floor in intensive care." Brandon watched his father put his arm around his mother as they started toward the elevators. He followed.

When the elevator doors opened on the third floor Brandon saw Sandra and Cheryl, his cousins, sitting in the waiting room. Cheryl, fourteen years old, was reading a book. Sandra, twelve, looked up when the elevator doors opened. Aunt Marie, his mother's sister, was talking with the Minister of the church where Grandpa was a member. When Brandon's mother walked into the waiting area his aunt Marie came over and hugged her and they began talking. Brandon went over to a chair by his cousin Sandra and sat down. He looked over at her.

"How long have you guys been here?"

"Since One this morning. Grandpa had a heart attack."

"I know," Brandon said. "Mom and Dad told me."

"He's real old," Cheryl said.

"Sixty is not real old," Brandon said. Cheryl frowned and went back to reading her book.

Marie led the way down the hall to the Nurse's Station, spoke quietly to the nurse and then went back to the waiting room. The nurse stood and escorted Kathleen and Ray to her father's room.

"One moment," she said at the door. She stepped into Buck Anderson's room, after a moment she reappeared. "You can go in now."

Kathleen stepped into the room quietly. Ray followed. Her father was lying on his back with his eyes closed. She laid her hand on his arm. He stirred then opened his eyes and looked at Kathleen and smiled and then glanced at Ray and nodded. Ray took his hand and shook it gently.

"Kate," Buck said, "you're here. Is Brandon with you?"

"Yes, he is," Kathleen said, wiping her eyes. Buck glanced at Ray then back to Kathleen.

"Kathleen, I need to talk to you for a moment."

Ray leaned forward and touched her father's hand, nodded, and looked at Kathleen. "I'll be in the waiting room," he said quietly and then left the room and closed the door.

Kathleen looked at her father expectantly. He smiled and placed his left hand on top of hers. "There's something very important I want to tell you. You probably know I won't be leaving here. I don't have very long."

"Daddy, don't say that."

"Listen to me. Your mother has been gone for over a year and now my time is here." Kathleen blinked moist eyes and listened. Her father took a breath.

"There's something I want you to do for me. You know that trunk in the hall closet that goes to you when I'm gone?"

"Yes, I know."

"Inside it there's a metal box. I want you to put it away and keep it. Then, when Brandon turns twenty-five, give it to him."

Kathleen nodded. "What is it?"

"It's a key to a safety deposit box. The address of the bank is in the box. In the safety deposit box there's a Keepsake that I want him to have when he's a man. Promise me that you will keep this to yourself until Brandon is twenty-five. Then I want you to give it to him."

Kathleen blinked and nodded.

"*Promise me*," Buck Anderson said lifting his head. Kathleen held her father's eyes for a moment.

"I promise, Daddy," she said.

Buck Anderson grimaced in pain….

Chapter 3

THE GIFT

Houston, Texas

Brandon Lee Stevens pulled the thumbtack out of the wall and tossed the spent calendar into the trashcan. Glancing around the desktop, he located the letter opener, picked it up, and punctured the plastic wrap on the new one. Removing the wrap, he held it up and looked at it. At the top, in crisp early American style, the numbers read *1998*. Just below it covering the top half of the calendar was an artist rendition of a sleek nineteen ninety-eight Ford Taurus, bright red. He inserted the thumb tack through the small hole provided, then located it in the same spot, and pushed the tack in firmly.

Brandon, still a little foggy from the New Year's Eve party, stood and went into the kitchen to refill his coffee. Audrina was up and pouring herself a cup.

"Good morning, Sweetheart," he said as he slid his arm around her waist. She moaned and leaned into him. "Some party, eh?" he added.

"Yeah," she said and took a sip of coffee. Brandon picked up the morning paper and Audrina picked up the remote and turned on the TV.

Brandon, six foot one, a hundred and eighty pounds, light brown hair and dark brown eyes, a graduate of the University of Texas at Arlington, was in his second year with the Houston Robotics Development Company. His training in computer science, specializing in robotics, won him a position at the Houston based company. Audrina, Brandon's find at a college party, five foot seven, a hundred and thirty pounds, brunette with brown eyes, became his wife upon graduation. Audrina was in her second year with Motion Tech Industries specializing in microelectronics.

Brandon and Audrina, a year earlier, purchased an older place on 5 aces in the country and were enjoying renovating it.

Brandon had finished the paper and joined Audrina watching the New Year's Day parade when the phone rang. Brandon picked it up.

"Brandon," he heard his mother say.

"Hi, Mom, happy New Year." Brandon listened as his mother reminded him that this was the year that he would spend his birthday at home with her. She had reminded him every year of the twenty-fifth birthday, to be spent at her house, since he was twelve.

"I remember, Mom," Brandon said. "I'll be there on June 2, the day I turn twenty-five, I promise." Brandon talked with his mother for a few minutes then his father came on the line and they talked. When his mother came back on the line, he handed the phone to Audrina and she and his mother talked at length.

Brandon thought about his mother's request; the request she had reminded him of every year on his birthday. It was so important to her that he remember. He'd quizzed her about it. Why his twenty-fifth birthday? She said it was a promise she had made to her father; his grandfather. When talking with her about it there was something in her eyes and voice that made him respect it. This year he would know. He would be twenty-five in June; June 2. He and Audrina had coined theories on what it might be. The intrigue was tantalizing. Audrina was wonderful. She and his mother had hit it off and visited on the phone often. Audrina had never attempted to pry into the sacred ground of birthday number twenty-five. Audrina was protecting the mystery—and enjoying it.

"This is the year," Audrina said as she hung up the phone.

"Yeah. This year we will know what Mom has kept to herself all these years. A promise she made to Grandpa Anderson. They were very close, Dad said, and, as you know, Grandpa died at sixty of a massive heart attack. When I asked Dad about the promise he said he didn't know. He left the hospital room so Grandpa and Mom could talk."

"Your mother's wonderful. She can keep a promise."

When June came around Brandon and Audrina arranged their vacations to begin on June 2 to keep his promise to be at his mother's on his birthday. They planned to leave Houston on Saturday, May 31 and drive to his parent's home, spend Sunday with them, then leave after the birthday party Monday, June 2.

Arlington, Texas

Sunday, June 1, Brandon slipped out of bed in the guest room at his parent's home. Audrina stirred then got quiet again. Brandon quietly dressed then walked down the familiar hallway to the kitchen. The light was on over the sink; the dim pattern cut a line across the carpet of the hallway. The glow of the coffee pot ready light caught his eye. Brandon quietly got a coffee cup off the wooden pegboard beside the cabinet and poured himself a cup of coffee, then went into the living room. His father was sitting in his recliner in the dark sipping a cup of coffee.

"Good morning, Son," Ray said.

"Good morning, Dad," Brandon responded then sat down in his mother's matching recliner. They sat in silence for some time with the quiet interrupted only by the ticking of the wall clock with its gold colored pendulum swinging one way each second. Brandon remembered looking up at it years earlier and wondering how they figured out how long to make the pendulum so the clock would keep accurate time. A curiosity that had never faded over the years. A curiosity that increased his pulse as he thought about tomorrow and the answer to a thirteen year wait. What was going to happen on birthday number twenty-five? Brandon glanced at his father.

"Dad, you still don't know about tomorrow?"

"Not a word, Son. But I can tell you this. Soon after your mother talked with your grandfather, he passed away. We spent that night with your Aunt Marie. On the way from the hospital to your Aunt Marie's house, your mother had me drive by your grandfather's house and pick up an old wooden trunk. We locked it in the trunk of the car and..."

"What was in it?" Brandon interrupted.

"Pictures, I guess. I know that one came out of it," Ray said pointing to the wall across the room. Brandon stood, turned on the light, and studied the picture. It was in black and white, mounted in an antique frame, with a bubble shaped glass over the image. There were two young boys dressed in overalls standing side by side with their arms hanging straight down. They were not smiling when the picture was taken. Ray stepped to Brandon's side.

"That's your grandfather, Buck, and his brother, your great uncle Robert. They were twelve and fourteen; your grandfather was the older." Brandon studied the picture for a moment then he and his father returned to their seats.

"Surely, Mom didn't wait thirteen years to give me a picture."

"I doubt it."

"Well," Brandon said, "I'll know tomorrow."

Birthday # 25

Monday, Brandon's birthday, his mother set the cake in the center of the table. Brandon blew out the twenty-five candles in one breath. His mother, father, and Audrina cheered and clapped their hands. Kathleen handed Brandon a knife and gestured toward the cake. Brandon cut four pieces and put them on plates. They enjoyed the cake and coffee, Brandon careful not to mention the promise.

The cake finished, Brandon announced that he and Audrina were anxious to start their vacation; pointing out that there were a lot of things they wanted to see in the two weeks. His mother smiled and left the room. A few minutes later, she returned with a metal box four inches square and two inches deep. It was a faded green color with the paint missing in some places and it had an emblem on the lid with scroll lettering advertising Stouffer's Candies. The box was sealed with a clear tape that had yellowed with age. His mother was gripping it with both hands and holding it to her

24

breast. Brandon, his father, and Audrina remained quiet.

"Brandon, this is from your grandfather. He made me promise not to tell anyone about it. He said to give it to you when you were twenty-five."

Brandon nodded awkwardly when she placed the box in his hands. Brandon hugged his mother. "I love you, Mom," he said quietly. She stepped back and nodded then looked at Audrina. Audrina hugged Kathleen then looked curiously at the faded metal box in Brandon hands.

Brandon sat down at the table and removed the yellowed tape sealing the lid onto the box. He looked up at the three watching him then pulled the lid off the box. Inside there was a business card with a key taped to the back of it and a sealed envelope folded in half lying on the bottom of the box under the business card. Brandon picked up the business card, looked at the key for a moment, at the number 113 stamped on it, then turned the card over and read it.

Wichita Falls Bank and Trust
1101 Main Street
Wichita Falls, Texas
Phone: BL3-1766

"This is a key to a safety deposit box in a bank in Wichita Falls," Brandon said. He picked up the envelope. Hand written across the front of it was: Brandon Lee Stevens. Brandon tore open the envelope, removed the sheet of paper, and unfolded it. It read:

Please give the contents of this safety deposit box to my grandson; Brandon Lee Stevens. He'll have the key. It's box number 113.

Buck Anderson

Brandon looked at his mother. "Do you know what's in the bank box?"

"Your grandfather said it was a Keepsake," his mother answered. "I don't know what it is but he said he wanted you to have it when you were a man."

"Grandpa knew how to create a mystery, didn't he?" Brandon said.

"It was very important to him; he made me promise just before he died."

"Did he say why he wanted me to be twenty-five before you could give it to me?"

"No. He said you had to be a man."

Chapter 4

THE LETTER

"Let's go see what it is and then head out on vacation," Brandon said. He saw Audrina nodding before he finished the sentence as they drove away from his parent's home.

"If it turns out to be just a family relic or heirloom that's fragile," Audrina said, "we won't spend our whole vacation wondering what it is."

Brandon smiled and glanced at her. "My feelings exactly."

They drove to Wichita Falls and got a room. Tuesday morning, they went to the bank at 9:00 a.m. Brandon and Audrina stepped up to the service desk and requested access to the safety deposit box.

"Your name and box number, Sir."

"I'm Brandon Lee Stevens. The box is in the name of my grandfather, Buck Anderson." Brandon handed the lady the note from the metal box and showed her the key. She read the note, looked up at Brandon, at Audrina, then back to the note. She got up from her desk, excused herself, and walked into the bank offices. A few moments later, she reappeared and escorted Brandon and Audrina into the bank president's office.

"Mr. Stevens," he said when Brandon walked into the office.

"Yes," Brandon said as they shook hands. "This is my wife, Audrina."

"I'm Herbert Simmons," the bank officer said as he shook Audrina's hand.

"Mr. Stevens, may I ask you for some identification?"

"Sure." Brandon took out his wallet and produced his driver's license. The president looked at it, returned it to Brandon, and smiled. He offered Brandon and Audrina a chair then sat down behind his desk. He picked up a file pocket, pulled the elastic band off and opened it.

"This box has been sealed for thirty-eight years. We have reviewed the documents every year. Mr. Anderson came into the bank in 1960 and reserved the box. He came in every year and paid the fee. Then in 1973, he came in and paid the fee through 1998. We haven't heard from him since." Brandon and Audrina looked at each other. The banker looked up and smiled.

"I was born in 1973," Brandon said. "Buck Anderson was my grandfather on my mother's side." Herbert Simmons nodded then reached into the file pocket and retrieved the bank key for box 113. He stood and walked into the safety deposit box area with Brandon and Audrina following him then inserted the key into the box. He nodded toward them then stepped outside the door. Brandon inserted his key then grasped the bank key then turned the two keys together and pulled the safety deposit box open. Audrina leaned close as Brandon lifted the metal lid. Inside was a drawstring pouch, blue velvet, twelve inches long and six inches wide. Brandon and Audrina looked at each other, and then Brandon reached into the box and picked it up.

"It feels like there's an envelope inside it…and something solid." Brandon started to open it. Audrina touched his arm.

"Let's go to the car."

Brandon nodded and closed the box.

Brandon started the car and turned on the air conditioning. The cool air filled the car in the warm mid-morning sunshine. He pulled the drawstring pouch open, reached in, and retrieved a yellow envelope. On the front, in his grandfather's handwriting was Brandon's full name. He laid it on his lap then reached into the pouch again and retrieved a golf ball sized sphere. It was a translucent smoky black color and seemed to have no weight. Brandon held it up above his other hand, palm open, and released the sphere. It floated slowly down to his open palm. He studied it for a moment then looked over at Audrina; her eyes met his. He tested the weight in his hand then handed to her. She tested the weight then turned it over and over in her hands, examining it. She held it up about a foot above her other hand and released it. It fell slowly. She tried it a second time. "It's almost weightless," she said carefully examining the surface.

Brandon picked up the envelope and removed the hand written pages then unfolded them.   Audrina followed along when Brandon began reading aloud.

June 2, 1973

Dear Brandon,

> *"You were born this morning. You are my first grandson. I never had a son to grow into a man and do this for me so it had to wait for you. The fact that you are reading this means that you are a man, twenty-five years old, and I'm gone. The year will be 1998 and you may have already met the people from the other planet..."*

Brandon recoiled then looked at Audrina. She looked at him as her mouth fell open. They looked at the letter again then Brandon continued reading aloud:

> *"If you have met them then you can ask them what this black ball is and what it's used for. If you haven't then maybe you can find*

out what it is yourself. I figure that in the year 1998 people will know a lot more that we do now.

First, I had better tell you where it came from. I was one of the soldiers that helped clean up the wreckage when those people crashed their spaceship in New Mexico. They are not as big as us; only about three or four feet tall. I saw three of them that were killed in the crash lying on a blanket. Anyway, I found this ball among the wreckage we were cleaning up. It was so light I wanted it for a Keepsake so I put it inside the bloused fold of my fatigues at the top of my boot. Nobody noticed and nobody knew I had it.

When we finished cleaning up the area, they took us back to the barracks then had a meeting with all of us that was on the cleanup detail. They warned us that what we had done was classified. If we told anybody, we would go

31

to prison. I was glad they didn't find out about the Keepsake. I would have been in a lot of trouble. Everybody that was on the cleanup crew was transferred to other bases. I was sent to California.

Now I want to tell you about the Keepsake. It's indestructible. I tried to break it open to see what was inside. I tried a hammer, saw, even a drill; nothing worked. I even tried a blowtorch. It didn't affect it at all. It must be made of some special stuff.

Well, that's all I know about it. I want you to have it. I sure hope it turns out to be something special because it was very special to me. I'm locking it away for you today."

Your grandfather,
Buck Anderson

Brandon and Audrina stared at the smooth black sphere.

"Grandpa Anderson was there; he saw it for himself," Brandon said.

"It takes my breath away to think about it," Audrina added. "For us to actually have a family member there who saw *it* and…*them*.

"It really happened, Audrina, and this is a piece of the spaceship. It's light as a feather but feels like metal. And, according to the letter, it's indestructible I wonder what it is and what was its use?"

Brandon placed it in Audrina's hand when she extended it, palm open. She studied it closely then held it next to her ear and shook it.

"Are you thinking what I'm thinking?" Brandon said.

"We've got two weeks," Audrina said then reached into the back seat and picked up the road Atlas. She handed it to Brandon. He opened it to New Mexico, studied it for a moment, and then turned the pages to Texas.

"We drive southwest through Lubbock, to Brownfield, then a hundred and thirty-four miles straight west to Roswell."

As Brandon drove out of Wichita Falls, he noticed the giant black metal *horses* rocking in slow motion, pumping the mixture of salt water and flakes of oil out of the North Central Texas ground. The mixture was pumped to nearby holding tanks where it would settle out; oil on top and water on bottom. The salt water was then pumped back into the ground then the crude oil drained from the tanks for a trip to the refinery, then to his and many other gas tanks. The *horses* had fascinated him when he was a child and they would come to Holiday, Texas to visit with his grandfather.

His mind went back to his grandfather's face as he remembered it. It was always gentle and understanding. He'd always looked at Brandon fondly and had praised him for the things he'd done. And, *all that time*....

Brandon wished he could see the spaceship, flying saucer, for himself, and the people that came to Earth in it; small, with big heads....

"You're awfully quiet," Audrina said.

"I was wondering what the spaceship looked like, and the Creatures that flew it."

"I believed it really happened; Roswell I mean, before we got this," Audrina said rolling the sphere between her fingers. "There's just too much inquiry into the event, too many witness that ring true, and too much nationwide interest in it. But since there has been consistent denial by the military all these years and so many different opinions of what the aliens were like I don't think we will ever know the real truth. It's really something that your grandfather was there; saw it, and got this to pass down through the years to you. We're lucky; for us it's verified. There's something special about knowing the real truth although it will probably make no difference in our lifetimes.

"It's an adventure," Brandon said.

"Yes, it is and I love it!" Audrina agreed.

Roswell, NM

Wednesday morning, 10:00 a.m., Brandon and Audrina drove into Roswell and stopped at a service station. Audrina dropped the Keepsake into her purse, zipped it closed, and went to the Ladies' Room. Brandon fueled the car, put on his best tourist's face, and asked directions to the famous Roswell UFO crash site. The attendant smiled warmly and pointed at a wire rack sitting on the end of the counter. Brandon picked up one of the mimeographed sheets of a hand-drawn map and directions to the UFO crash site. Printed in the middle of the sheet was *Debris Field*. Brandon thanked the attendant and went to the car. Audrina was just closing her door. Brandon got behind the wheel and handed the crude hand drawn map to Audrina. She studied the sheet with growing excitement as Brandon pulled the car back into traffic. She looked up.

"We take a right up ahead on Main Street then head north until we reach the road that goes left toward Corona. It's about an hour north of Roswell. Brandon made the turn then, minutes later, watched the last of the city pass behind them.

At precisely six miles north of Roswell the inside of Audrina's purse was filled with an eerie pink light, a flash of light emanating from the sphere that lasted only a millisecond.

When Brandon turned off the pavement onto the dirt road leading to the celebrated crash site another vehicle was coming out. Brandon stopped the car and rolled down his window. The bearded driver of a four-by-four pickup stopped and rolled down his window.

"You find anything?" Brandon said in a jovial manner."

"No, but I've been coming out here and looking or twelve years. You're almost there; it's just over the next hill." The man reached over to the right seat of his truck and picked up a magazine and handed to Brandon then pointed at the open page.

"Here's a picture of the crash site." Brandon accepted the magazine and he and Audrina studied the terrain pictured of the full page spread.

While they studied the scene, the sphere timed out and the flash occurred again, concealed by Audrina's closed purse.

"Thanks," Brandon said and handed the book back to the friendly driver. He drove away. Brandon glanced at Audrina then eased the car forward on the dirt road. Audrina unzipped her purse and retrieved the sphere. When they topped the hill Brandon stopped the car and he and Audrina got out. They shielded their eyes from the Sun and looked across the terrain.

"Looks like just another piece of the New Mexico desert doesn't it," Audrina said.

"It isn't though."

"No...no it isn't," Audrina agreed then walked out away from the car looking at the ground. Brandon followed and couldn't help doing the same thing although he knew that thousands of sets of eyes had thoroughly searched every square inch of the area. Everything from the size of the head of a match and up would have been picked up and examined; probably several times. And, no doubt, would be many more times by people who wanted to find something, anything at all, that would verify that it was real and it had really happened.

That something they desperately wanted had been given to Brandon on his birthday. Now he knew for real. He stopped and shielded his eyes again and looked at the surroundings far into the distance. To the south, miles away, was the Lincoln National Forest and Boy Scout Mountain. To the left, the town of Roswell and the site of the Roswell Army Air Field, now the Roswell airport. To the west was another mountain range. To the east, more desert, as well as to the north. Audrina stepped up to Brandon's side.

"If anything escaped being found it would just about have to be away from this area; maybe in one of those mountain ranges, or the forest." Audrina nodded, glanced at the sphere then dropped it in her purse and closed it. "You hungry?" she said looking up at Brandon.

He nodded. "Let's drive back into town, get a room, and go to lunch." They drove back to the main highway to Roswell and headed south into town.

At the six-mile mark, the sphere, passing out of range, turned off.

Chapter 5

THE UFO MUSEUM

Shortly after entering the city limits they spotted a Best Western motel, pulled into the drive, rented a room for three days, and unloaded the car. Minutes later, they were downtown in a restaurant. The waitress appeared, smiling warmly.

"What can I get you folks?" They placed their orders then Brandon said,

"...and could you tell me which way is it to the old Army Air Field?"

"Sure," she said and smiled again. "Lots of people ask about that. It's about seven miles south on Main Street. You'll drive straight into it. It's now called the Commercial Air Field. Also, if you're interested, the UFO museum is just down Main Street from here about half a block on your right."

"Thank you," Brandon said.

He turned to Audrina. "Let's stop by the museum on the way to the air field."

Audrina nodded. "Yes. I'd like to inquire about the crash." She opened her purse and picked up the sphere. "Do you think we should tell them about this?"

"No," Brandon said quickly. "There's no telling what that might stir up."

Audrina nodded. "They would jump on it, especially if we showed them the letter and told them about your grandfather's being there."

"I think we should just play the tourist roll for now and see what we can find out about 1947."

Audrina agreed. Brandon saw excitement in her eyes.

Brandon and Audrina walked the half block to the UFO Museum and Research Center and entered. There was a group of people gathered at the first exhibit. A museum guide turned from a six-foot-by-six-foot map of the Roswell area and began speaking.

"Ah, we're at the start of the tour," Audrina said. They hurried over to the group and joined them as the speaker began.

First, he explained the origin of the UFO Museum and Research Center, named its staff, one of which had been sixteen years old and lived in Roswell when the crash occurred. Then he turned to the map and pointed. *"This is Roswell. Up to the north about twenty-three miles is the Alleged Site featured in the Roswell movie. Then further north and left at the next intersection toward Corona is the Debris Field."*

Brandon looked at the area the guide was indicating. It was the site he and Audrina had visited earlier. The guide continued; *"It is our contention that there were two saucers. During the electrical storm on that fateful weekend, one of the ships was hit by lightning, which caused it to collide with its sister ship. The impact of the two ships caused their outer hulls to explode; the debris raining down causing the debris field near Corona. Following the accident, the two ships flew several miles before impacting the ground. One flew about twenty miles and impacted a rain gully north of Roswell, now known as the Alleged Site. The other flew some thirty-two miles and came down in the Lincoln National Forest close to a camp ground due south of the Debris Field."* Brandon and Audrina looked at each other.

"My God," Brandon said, "there were two spaceships—saucers. They ran into each other and then crashed."

Audrina nodded. "We saw only part of the crash site, or sites. We've got to visit the other two; the actual sites where the ships hit."

The speaker continued. *"Where the second ship came down was just off Old Pine Lodge Road in the Lincoln National Forest. In 1947, it was Highway 48; now it's Highway 246, however, it's still known as Old Pine Lodge Road. At the time the saucer crashed there was a couple camping just fifty yards away. They were there partying for the Fourth of July weekend. They saw the bright flash of light when the ships exploded then saw the ship coming at them. It cut a swath through the trees as it came in. It hit a huge rock, about the size of an automobile and cracked it in half then came to rest leaning up against it.*

"That couple was an oil field worker named James Ragsdale and his girlfriend. They made their way through the woods to the impact site and

found that the violent collision with the huge rock ruptured the craft. It ripped a hole in the spaceship large enough to actually get inside.

"Mr. Ragsdale passed away on July 1, 1995. On June 26th, a few days before his death, he allowed us to make a video about the event. We also have a book containing his story."

"We have to get that video and the book," Brandon said.

The group moved to the next exhibit. Brandon and Audrina followed. When they passed a divider, they saw, behind a large picture window, a hospital bed with a figurine of an alien lying on it and a mannequin dressed in surgical garb standing at the end of the bed. The figurine was identical to the Roswell Movie's depiction of the alien's appearance. Brandon experienced a solemn moment as he looked at the scene. *"This scene was donated to the UFO Museum and Research Center by the Producer of the Roswell movie."* Brandon raised his hand. The guide pointed at him and raised his eyebrows.

"Did Mr. Ragsdale see this?" *"No. I wish he could have seen it. I would like to know how close it is to the real appearance and size."* Brandon nodded. The guide continued his speech as Brandon and Audrina studied the small figurine. Brandon was staring at the abdomen of the three and a half feet long representation of the alien when the guide's voice again captured his ears…"*—navel. We don't know if that's a true representation but if it is, it has implications on how…"* Brandon leaned close to Audrina's ear.

"They may be very different from us." The group moved on through the tour. Brandon glanced into the video viewing room when the guide pointed it out to the group. When the tour finished the group of people dispersed to different parts of the museum. Brandon and Audrina walked slowly around the walls looking at all the displays, photographs, and paintings. A rack of flyers was sitting by one of the displays. The sign indicated they were free. One of them titled EBE caught Brandon's eye. He picked it up. Half an hour later, they were standing in front of a rack full of books and video tapes.

Brandon picked up the book and the video. He paid the cashier then asked if the viewing room was available. The lady gestured toward it and smiled. He and Audrina went into the viewing room, seated themselves, opened the 'Ragsdale Story' and began to read. Fifteen minutes later, they looked at each other.

"This guy is for real," Audrina said. "Oh, I envy him." Brandon nodded then stepped up to the big screen TV and inserted the video. Following the credits and some testimonials concerning Roswell and James Ragsdale the image of an old man filled the screen. There were two other people standing as his bedside. The old man began to talk and answer questions as one who was not schooled in presentations on camera. He spoke in his own language etiquette and mannerisms. Brandon eyes widened. His gut told him that he was hearing the truth. A truth with serious implications. He glanced at Audrina; she was caught up in the video. When it finished she turned toward Brandon.

"It's true. One of the saucers came down in the Lincoln National Forest. It flew that far after the explosion."

"Let's talk to one of the staff and get directions to the Ragsdale site. We can drive out there in the morning." Brandon spotted an older white haired man greeting people as they came into the Research Center. Brandon approached and asked directions. He stepped around the counter and returned with a copy of a hand drawn map. The staff member briefly explained the map. Brandon then asked another question:

"Where do I turn off the road to the Alleged Site?" The gentleman gave the directions then smiled again.

"Thank you," Brandon said. "This is a nice museum; we enjoyed our visit."

"We've had visitors from all over the world in the last three years." Brandon nodded and shook hands with the older man then he and Audrina went out the door and onto the sidewalk. Brandon looked back toward the restaurant and their parked car.

"Let's go back to the motel and digest this information." Audrina nodded. They returned to their car. Brandon started it then looked at the flyer titled EBE. Audrina noticed. They read it together. "It says that an alien survived until '52," Brandon said, "and an Entomologist was taken to examine him. The guy gave him the name EBE."

"I heard about that," Audrina added. "Extraterrestrial Biological Entity."

Brandon and Audrina sat on the motel bed leaning up against the headboard reading the italicized words from the Ragsdale book again. The words that James Ragsdale himself spoke during the final interview.

"Considering the way the Roswell Incident happened and the cover up that followed, this man was very lucky," Audrina said. "He just happened to be where one of the ships came down and got to see it and to see the aliens; the *people from the other planet* as your grandfather put it."

"Ragsdale called them *little people* about three or four feet tall," Brandon offered. "He said they were gray skinned and he actually touched one of them and the skin felt like a wet snake, a reptilian feel. He said he tried to pull off one of the crew's helmet and couldn't because it fit too tight. Was it because it wasn't a helmet but was an exoskeleton? That would mean they have insectoid attributes. Big eyes, he said; that's insect type. And something else, there was no windshield or windows in the ship. If those larger eyes had a much broader spectrum of vision than we do, say, including the x-ray band, they could see through the wall of the ship. No windshield needed. No wonder that the people that dealt with the discovery were frightened enough to think the public was not ready for such a revelation. There are also claims that they, the aliens, did not use

45

voice communication as we do; it was in that movie; they used telepathy instead. That would be scary."

Audrina was quiet for a moment. "This is getting serious."

Thursday morning, following breakfast, they headed north on Main street.

"There it is," Brandon said when he saw the sign: *Pine Lodge Road*.

While Brandon waited for clearance to make the left turn, Audrina leaned forward and looked down the street then opened her purse and retrieved the sphere. Brandon looked at it then made the turn when the traffic cleared. He drove slowly until he was out of the city and then increased his speed on the blacktop road. Soon he came to a *Y* in the road. A sign indicated Hwy 256 was to the right; Brandon followed it. Audrina had the sphere in her hand with the hand laying in her lap. She was scanning the view out the windshield.

The proximity sequence inside the sphere, passing in range, initiated and it flashed.

Audrina's eyes snapped to the sphere for a few seconds then to Brandon.

"Did you see that?"

"What?"

"A flash of light!" she said holding up the sphere. Bandon's eyes snapped to the sphere for a few seconds then he looked back through the windshield and corrected the car's direction. He pulled over to the side of the road and stopped the car. He picked up the sphere from Audrina's hand and stared at it.

"It flashed?" Brandon said excitedly.

"Yeah! It was a pink light. I was looking around when I saw a flash of a pinkish colored light."

They sat on the side of the road for several minutes watching the sphere. Brandon shook it. It remained its well-known smoky black color.

"Maybe the flash you saw was a piece of broken glass beside the road or something."

"No, it was inside the car." They watched the Keepsake a few more minutes; it remained inert, then Brandon glanced at Audrina.

"Let's put in on the dash so we can see it and continue on to the crash site." Audrina nodded. Brandon placed the sphere on the center of the dash. It rolled to the passenger side of the car. Audrina opened her purse, pulled out a Kleenex, folded it four times then placed it on the center of the dash. Brandon put the Keepsake on it. It remained in place. He steered the car back onto the road and resumed highway speed. As the miles rolled by, every few seconds, Brandon glanced at the sphere. Anticipation began to build in him as he kept up the vigil of watching the road and the sphere at the same time. An oncoming car pulled his attention from the Keepsake for a few moments. As soon and the car was clear he resumed his vigil.

Inside the sphere the timed proximity sequence reset and the flash occurred again.

Brandon was looking straight at it when it happened. He slammed on the brakes and the car skidded to a stop sitting at an angle in the road. Audrina braced herself on the dash as the Road Atlas and her purse went into the floor. The sphere rolled off the Kleenex and to the right side of the car. Brandon reached and picked it up.

"I saw it!" he said.

"I did, too!" A car pulled up behind them. The driver honked the horn. Brandon looked through the right hand mirror then pulled the car onto the shoulder of the road. The driver pulled up beside them and looked through his right hand window.

"You folks okay?"

"Yes," Brandon said. "I just dropped something. Thanks for stopping." The driver nodded, smiled, and then drove away. Brandon looked at the sphere then at Audrina. Her eyes met his.

"Do you know what this means!" Brandon said. "There's something still here and this is connected to it somehow."

Audrina picked up the sphere from Brandon's hand and examined the surface again. "Whatever it is has waited for fifty years,"

Brandon nodded.

"I wonder if what's on the other end knows we are here?" Audrina added. Bandon sat back in the seat for a moment.

"That's a good question," he said, and then muttered: "Grandpa, what have you gotten us into?" He looked at Audrina. "Let's drive on to the crash site. Maybe this will lead us to it; whatever it is."

"Brandon," Audrina said acutely, "this could be very serious."

"I've got to know," Brandon said. Audrina was quiet for a few moments.

"Me, too. How often do you think it flashes?" Brandon looked at her and blinked then looked at the sphere then his watch. Audrina looked at hers.

"How long since you saw it flash the first time?"

"About thirty or forty minutes," Audrina said. "But that may not be the first time it's flashed. It may be just the first time we saw it. It's been in my purse most of the time." Brandon looked at Audrina then looked down, blinking his eyes in thought.

"I wonder how long it's been flashing. It wasn't flashing in Wichita Falls or on the way here. We had it out in the open almost all the time then. It didn't start flashing until we got here." Brandon and Audrina looked at each other, then stared at each other's eyes for a few seconds then shouted in unison:

"Proximity!"

"It's a proximity device!" Brandon said loudly.

"Yeah," Audrina said, "and we're close enough to activate it. It's 9:45 a.m. right now. It flashed about five minutes ago. That means that it's about half an hour between flashes." Audrina opened her purse and took out a writing pad and a pen then looked at her watch again.

"Five minutes ago would be 9:40," she said and noted the time on the pad. "Let's sit here until it flashes again and check how long between flashes." Brandon nodded then placed the sphere back on the dash. They watched the Keepsake anticipating the next flash of light.

"Just think," Brandon said, "all the years that Grandpa had it that he never knew about the flashes. He must have found it and concealed it on his person between flashes. Then when they finished the cleanup and went back to Roswell, it was out of range. What a monumental coincidence. If it had flashed the military would have quickly taken it and went about doing what we are doing right now."

"Your grandfather must have never brought it out here."

"To him if was a special souvenir."

"It's more, a lot more." They were silent for a time. A few minutes later the flash occurred again. They had their eyes on the sphere when it happened. The light originated deep inside the sphere, radiated to the surface, then a pink flash occurred. Brandon blinked several times then looked at his watch. Audrina checked the time.

"It's 10:06," Audrina said. "Twenty-six minutes! We must be getting closer."

"Let's drive on to the crash site," Brandon said excitedly. He steered the car back onto the road and proceeded toward the turnoff outlined on the map.

"There's the sign," Audrina said. It read: *Boy Scout Mountain*. He looked ahead and saw the turnoff as described by the white haired gentleman at the museum. Brandon slowed the car and made the turn. Driving slowly along the rocky dirt road he glanced at the sphere every few seconds. A few minutes later he eased the car to a stop and picked up the mimeographed page of the map and studied it.

"Okay," he said. "We need to look for a microwave tower on the left. Just past it is the turn to the crash site." Audrina picked up the sphere from the dash and held it in her hand as they began the vigil of watching for the microwave tower among the trees. A few minutes later Audrina pointed through the windshield to the left.

"There it is." Brandon saw parts of the tower in between the trees. Shortly the intersection appeared and he made the turn, and then stopped the car.

"The map says we should park here and walk the last quarter mile or so unless we have a four-wheel drive vehicle." Brandon studied the road surface. "The road looks good enough to drive on a little farther." Audrina looked at the road and nodded then checked her watch. She held the sphere up then checked her watch again then frowned.

"What?" Brandon said.

"It's already been twenty-six minutes and it hasn't flashed," Audrina said. Brandon looked at his watch.

"Twenty-seven minutes," he said then picked up the sphere from Audrina's hand. They were silent as they watched it. One minute later it flashed. Audrina breathe a sigh of relief then checked the time.

"Twenty-eight minutes," she said. "We're farther away from it."

"That doesn't make sense," Brandon said and then started the car forward again. A four-wheel drive Jeep Waggoneer appeared and came toward them on the road ahead. Brandon steered to the side of the road and stopped. The Waggoneer pulled up beside them. A middle-aged lady rolled down her window and smiled. Brandon rolled down his window.

"You been to the crash site?"

"I drove by it. I drove the jeep trail from Arabella."

"I was wondering about the road," Brandon said.

"They have graded it up to the crash site. You can drive all the way to it now if you watch the ruts and where you put your tires. There's a couple of places where she may have to get out and watch for you but you can make it. You'll know when you get to it. There's a mining road that goes off to the right and the campsite is right there on the left."

Brandon nodded and smiled. The lady drove away.

Brandon steered the car back onto the road and drove on slowly carefully negotiating the chug holes and rocks sticking out of the road's surface. Moments later Audrina pointed.

"There's the mining road." Brandon pulled the car over to the side of the road again and parked.

"Let's walk from here," he said. "It's only fifty yards or so."

They arrived at the circle of rocks on the left side of the road then looked at each other. Audrina was holding the Keepsake in her hand. Brandon extended his and she put it in his hand.

"How long since it flashed?" he said.

"Twenty-one minutes." Brandon looked at it and frowned.

"I thought it would be blinking like crazy when we got here."

"I did, too." They stepped over to the circle of rocks with the darkened area inside, squatted down and touched a couple of them, waiting for the next flash. A few minutes later it occurred. Audrina checked the time.

"Twenty-eight minutes," she said. "The time is still the same."

"Let's go find the place where the saucer hit," Brandon said. They stood then started toward the impact site, ducking under low hanging branches and carefully stepping over scattered underbrush on a surface scattered with pine needles and the shedding's of the cedar trees.

"Have you noticed that there are no trails?" Brandon said.

"Yeah," Audrina said nodding. "Apparently not very many people have visited this site."

"I doubt if very many people know about the Ragsdale site. We didn't know about it until we visited the museum." They looked at each other for a moment then hurried on to the huge rock that had been cracked in half as pictured in the book of the Ragsdale story. Brandon held the sphere close to the rock then touched it with it. It remained inert. He held it up in the air and waved it around. The sphere remained dark.

"Whatever is transmitting to it isn't here," Brandon said.

"Think about it," Audrina pointed out. "If it was here the military would have it now."

"Yeah, they would," Brandon agreed. They searched the area for an hour on the ground, in the trees, and among the rocks, hoping for something tantalizing. The sphere had flashed two more times; each time the flashes were exactly twenty-eight minutes apart.

"Let's think for a minute," Brandon said. "The time between flashes was shorter over on the highway north of where we are now."

"The Debris Field and the Alleged Site are both north of us, relatively speaking, from where we are now," Audrina said.

"But it didn't flash when we were there," Brandon said. They were silent for a moment. Audrina looked from the sphere to Brandon's face.

"Maybe it was flashing and we just didn't see it. I had it in my purse until we got there. We were there for about twenty or thirty minutes. When we decided to drive back to Roswell and eat I dropped it back in my purse again."

Brandon blinked and nodded. "What a coincidence. Let's get methodical about this. Let's go back to the highway, park by the sign that's close to the turnoff, and time the flashes exactly. Then go to the other site and time the flashes then go to the Debris Field and time the flashes."

Chapter 6

COORDINATES

Brandon and Audrina sat on the side of Old Pine Lodge Road near the turnoff to the Ragsdale Site and waited for the sphere to flash. Brandon took the writing pad and started a new sheet. At the top of the sheet he wrote: *Proximity Timing.* Then he dropped down on the sheet and wrote, *Ragsdale Site – 28 minutes.* He placed the sphere on the dash and they watched it until it flashed. He checked the time then they leafed through the Ragsdale book while waiting for the next timed sequence to emanate from it. Twenty-six minutes later it happened. Brandon checked the time. Then on the next line of the pad he wrote: *Highway sign north of the Ragsdale Site – 26 minutes,*

"Okay," he said. "Let's go to the next site." They drove back to Roswell on the Old Pine Lodge Road. Nearing the city, just before they arrived at the *Y*, the next flash occurred. When it happened Audrina checked the time.

"Fifty-three minutes," she said. "We're much farther away."

A few moments later the proximity mechanism inside the sphere, passing out of range, turned off.

When they reached the main highway Brandon turned left and headed for the crash site of the second saucer. At the six mile mark the sequence initiated again.   When the sphere flashed Audrina checked her watch.

"Twelve minutes!" she exclaimed. Brandon glanced at the sphere then pulled the car over to the side of the road and stopped.

"That doesn't make any sense," he said. "How could we suddenly be that much closer?" Audrina glanced at their notes.

Ragsdale Site – 28 minutes
Highway, north of Ragsdale Site – 26 minutes
Driving back to Roswell – 53 minutes
Driving away from Roswell – 12 minutes

She stared at the note for a moment then her eyes went to Brandon. "We drove out of, then back in, its range. This is a proximity device with a limited range, remember?" Brandon nodded then made a u turn and drove back to the intersection of Old Pine Lodge Road then made another u turn. He began the trip to the second site again. Seven minutes later the flash occurred. He braked the car and pulled over to the side of the road again.

"This is the perimeter," he said. "Now if we knew the range it has...." They looked at each other, then Brandon pulled back onto the road and proceeded to the second crash site. It was listed in the book as the Alleged Site. He made the turn then followed the winding road through the pasture as described to him. He passed over a cattle guard installed in the road, then another. He went down through a low place then up to two columns that had been erected at the site.

There was a cable strung on each side of the walkway from the two columns to the crash site dramatized in the Roswell movie. He and Audrina made the walk then approached the cliff where the disc had impacted. When they walked up to it they saw a block of what appeared to be red granite or sandstone. It was a three-foot-high block with a polished face three-by-four feet. There was an inscription carved into it. Brandon and Audrina leaned closer. It read:

WE DON'T KNOW WHO THEY WERE
OR WHERE THEY CAME FROM
WE DON'T KNOW WHY THEY CAME
ALL WE KNOW IS
THAT THEY CHANGED FOREVER
OUR PERCEPTION OF THE UNIVERSE
THIS FOREVER SACRED PLACE
IS DEDICATED JULY 1997 TO THE BEINGS
THAT MET THEIR DESTINIES
HERE JULY 1947

The Keepsake flashed. Audrina caught her breath then looked at Brandon.

"Write down the time," Brandon said.

Audrina looked at her watch and noted the time. She looked at the inscription again. "I didn't know that this site had been dedicated to...."

"The people from the other planet," Brandon finished.

"And it's dramatized for *us*," Audrina said. "We know where this sphere came from and what it means when it flashes." They looked around for a few minutes. Then as more time passed, they began watching the sphere constantly. Half an hour later Audrina looked at her watch again and took a breath.

"It's been thirty minutes and it hasn't flashed," she said, "we must be farther from it. Let's look around some more while we are waiting." Brandon nodded. They walked around the area, keeping the sphere in sight, looking at the ground. They walked down through the wash and up to the cliff on the other side supposedly to the exact spot where the disc had impacted fifty-one years earlier. Brandon tried to make out an impression in the cliff that would be a tell-tell sign that something had hit the cliff of dirt but was unable to outline any distinct imprint. He put his hands on his sides and surveyed the area all around the site.

"I'll bet people have been all over this ground with metal detectors."

"No doubt," Audrina agreed then looked at her watch again. "It's been an hour since it's flashed. Do you think that maybe we are out of range here?"

"Maybe, but let's wait a while longer and be sure. They sat down cross-legged on the ground and waited, watching the sphere. Twelve minutes later the precisely timed flash occurred.

"I can't get over the look of the mechanics of the flash," Brandon said. "When it comes on the sphere looks transparent then the point of light expands and fills its volume and then it flashes. It makes me gasp for breath each time I see it." Brandon took out the pad and noted the time: 3:47 p.m. He compared the times, did the numbers, and then looked at Audrina.

"Seventy-two minutes. We're much farther from it here." He noted the location and time on the pad. "Okay, let's drive back to the Debris Field and check the time there." They went to the car and made the drive to the first crash site they visited when they first arrived in Roswell. Sitting in the car they waited for and recorded the flash time: 4:55 p.m. then began the wait for the next sequence. Brandon reached into the back seat, dug through his overnight bag and came out with the letter from his Grandpa. He read it again, passing away the time. At 5:31 the flash occurred. Brandon logged the time.

"Thirty-six minutes," he said. "We're closer here. Let's go back to the motel, take these figures, and draw up a map."

"We can go by a store and pick up some paper, a ruler, a compass, a protractor, and a calculator," Audrina said. Brandon nodded and pulled the car into gear.

"There's a Kmart," Audrina said pointing. Bandon steered the car into the parking lot. They went in, picked up the supplies, and returned to the car. Brandon glanced at the sunset enhancing Captain's Peak.

"It's almost dark," Brandon said. "Let's get some dinner then go to the motel and work on a map." They went back to the same restaurant, got a table, and placed their orders. When the waitress withdrew Audrina sat staring at Brandon for a moment. He noticed.

"What?"

"It's early," Audrina said. "When we finish the map let's check out some of the night life in Roswell. Just to see what it's like," she added.

Brandon reached across the table and clasped her hands. "Okay. Say, let's see if there's a club or a dance that was here when Grandpa was here and coming to town on Saturday nights."

"Yeah, that will be fun."

When the waitress brought their drinks and salads Brandon made an inquiry: "My wife and I were wondering if there's a club here in Roswell that was here back in the forties when the Army Air Field was here."

"Oh, I don't know," she answered then glanced at an older lady sitting at the cash register. "Let me get Gertie. She's been here all her life; she would know." The waitress hurried over and spoke to the lady at the cash register then went back to her duties. The lady turned a key on the register, removed it, and then walked over to Brandon and Audrina's table. She laid her hand on Brandon's shoulder and spoke in a deep voice, raspy with age.

"What is it you want to know, Honey," she said. Brandon looked down for a moment and blinked at the familiarity, then looked back to the wrinkled face with dominate lipstick.

"I'm Brandon Stevens and this is my wife, Audrina." The lady looked at Audrina, smiled, and spoke in a man's voice.

"Hi, Sweetheart, I'm Gertie Wells." Audrina nodded and smiled.

"We were wondering if there's a club still in business here in Roswell that was here in the forties," Brandon said.

"Are you two good dancers?" Brandon and Audrina looked at each other.

"Pretty good," Audrina said.

"I love to dance," Gertie said. "The Desert Cactus is out toward the base or where the base was. The base was there then and the Desert Cactus was a hopping place. I kicked up my heels every Saturday night with those soldier boys. The place was packed every weekend."

Brandon picked up on the music in her voice and smiled. "My Grandpa, Buck Anderson, was stationed at the Roswell Army Air Field in the forties. Do you remember ever meeting him or maybe dancing with him?"

"Oh, no, Darling, I'm sorry, I don't. That was a long time ago and I danced with all the soldiers. I was pretty back then and they kept me busy." Gertie's eyes were sparkling behind a wrinkled and tired face.

"You're pretty now," Brandon said, "I hear it in your voice."

There was a reaction on the seventy-year-old face. "Oh, don't be silly," Gertie said playfully slapping Brandon on the shoulder. Gertie glanced at Audrina. Audrina winked that woman-to-woman endorsement. A smile formed on Gertie's lips.

"You two go on out there. The place has really slowed down; it's mostly middle-aged folks now, but it's nice." Gertie patted Brandon and Audrina on the shoulders and returned to her cash register.

"She's wonderful isn't she," Brandon said.

"I'll bet she was a *corker* back in the forties."

Back in their motel room, Brandon and Audrina cleared the round table that was sitting between the bed and the window with its two straight back chairs. Brandon laid out the Ragsdale book, turned it to the page with the county map, and studied it for a moment. The three crash sites were clearly labeled at the spots where they had taken the timing information with the sphere and its flash sequences.

He laid a sheet of copy paper over the map and pressed it down firmly then traced the points onto it. Then at the edge of the sheet, he drew an arrow up the page and labeled it *NORTH*. Further, he labeled the points *Debris Field of the Two Saucers as Crash Site of Saucer # 1* and *Crash Site of Saucer #2*. The Debris Field of the two saucers was the first crash site they visited upon arrival in Roswell. The crash site of saucer #1 was the Ragsdale Site. The crash site of saucer #2 was the Alleged Site as they were laid out on the county map featured in the Ragsdale book.

Audrina studied the sheet of copy paper and nodded. Brandon then laid the ruler on the sheet of paper, lined it up on the points of the Debris Field and the Ragsdale Site, and drew a line from one point to the other. "That's thirty-two miles."

He then laid the pad with the timing information on it onto the table beside the traced map and looked at it.

It read:
Proximity Timing

Ragsdale Site   -   28 minutes
Highway Sign, north of Ragsdale Site- 26 minutes
Alleged Site   -   72 minutes
Debris Field   -   36 minutes

"Okay," he said. "We know it's north of the Ragsdale Site because the flashes were closer together when we timed them north of the site itself."

Audrina nodded watching intensely then offered an observation: "The time from the Ragsdale Site to whatever it is, is twenty-eight minutes. And the time from the Debris Field to it is thirty-six minutes. That's sixty-four minutes."

Brandon nodded. They were silent for a moment, then looked at each other.

"The distance from one site to the other is thirty-two miles," Brandon said. "That's two minutes a mile!" Brandon picked up the ruler, laid it on their traced map, and measured from one point to the other.

"Four inches," he said. "Divide four inches by thirty-two miles." Audrina picked up the calculator; her fingers were quick.

"Point one-two-five; one-eight inch—one-eight is a mile." She looked at the Proximity List again. "Twenty-eight minutes at two minutes a mile would be fourteen miles." Brandon picked up the compass and squinted his eyes.

"Fourteen miles with one-eight inch for each mile is one and three-quarter inches." He quickly set the protractor then placed the metal point on the Ragsdale Site and drew an arc across the line he scribed from the Debris Field to the Ragsdale Site. Audrina picked up the calculator.

"Thirty-six minutes at the Debris Field is two and one-quarter inches," she said. Brandon drew the second arc. The two arcs met at a single point on the site-to-site line. They looked at each other.

"That's where it is!" Brandon said. "It's fourteen miles north of the Ragsdale Site and eighteen miles south of the Debris Field, which is the same place."

"Let's double-check it," Audrina said. "Let's check the time from the Alleged Site." Brandon nodded, picked up the compass, and watched Audrina on the calculator.

"It's four and a half inches," she said. Brandon set the protractor and drew the arc. They watched it pass through the point where the other two arcs met.

"That's it," Brandon said. "That's the location." Brandon hurried to the car and got the road atlas then returned to the room. He and

Audrina studied the area on the Mew Mexico state map.

"It's open desert," Brandon said. "Why didn't they find it?"

"Maybe it's underground," Audrina said. Brandon thought for a moment then put his hand on Audrina's shoulders.

"Let's charter a plane in the morning and fly over the area. We know exactly where to look. Maybe there will be something there. Also we can check out the roads from the air and see how close we can get in the car."

Audrina went to the bathroom to freshen up. Brandon studied the map again and the road atlas. When she reappeared, he looked up then took her in his arms.

"Let's go to the Desert Cactus for a while," he said. Audrina smiled then mimicked dancing. Brandon opened the door for her.

"There it is," Audrina said, pointing to the right. "Looks like about twenty cars in the parking lot." Brandon steered the car into it and parked. They went into the club, found a table, and ordered drinks. The club was patronized by mostly middle-aged couples, some with single sons or daughters accompanying them. Brandon saw four other younger couples. The atmosphere was friendly and relaxing. The dance floor was forty-by-fifty feet. Brandon, looking around the perimeter, noticed that their table and many of the others were on the edge of a once enormous dance floor.

Pool tables had been added around the outside walls. The stage would accommodate a sizable band but tonight there was a lone disc jockey behind a half moon table, playing records. Three couples were dancing.

"Where's the Keepsake?" Brandon said.

"In my bra." Brandon recoiled and his mouth fell open.

"Well, I'm not going to leave it in my purse on the table while we are dancing."

"I hope it doesn't start flashing."

Audrina held Brandon's eyes for a long moment. Brandon saw a trace of a seductive look. "We're out of range."

"Let's dance," Brandon said then stood and extended his hand. Audrina placed her hand in his then stood. They walked out of the dance floor and faced each other.   Brandon glanced at her cleavage then into her eyes then pulled her into his arms. They danced to two songs then returned to the table.

Brandon picked up his drink and took a sip looking around at the club again. He glanced at Audrina's breast again then to her eyes. She raised her eyebrows.   He smiled then looked toward the bar. His eyes met the eyes of a man in his seventies. The man was staring at Brandon. Brandon held his eyes for a moment then looked back at Audrina.

"There's an older man at the bar staring at us." Audrina looked toward the bar. The man met her eyes for a moment then looked back at Brandon.

"Wonder who he is," Audrina said.

"I don't know. I've never seen him before."

"Come on," Audrina said getting up from the table and starting for the bar, carrying her drink. Brandon followed. She walked over to the older man then sat down on the barstool. Brandon took the stool beside her.

"Hi," Audrina said. "I noticed you looking at us. Have we met?"

"Oh, no," the man said warmly. "Your fella' reminds me of one of the soldiers that used to come here."

Brandon sat straight up on his bar stool. "My Grandpa, Buck Anderson, was stationed here in 1947, did you know him?"

"No," he said. "I never knew any of the boys. Back then, I was waiting tables. A lot of the boys came in here and met the girls. The place was packed every weekend. There was one young soldier that stood out. He went around this dance floor like a born dancer. Danced with every girl in the place. You," the man said, pointing, "dance just like him. He was the life of the party. Always laughing and funning with everybody. Son, you're the spittin' image of him."

"That had to be my Grandpa Anderson," Brandon said. The old man nodded.

"Is he still living?"

"No, Sir," Brandon said. "He passed away in 1985; heart attack." The older man looked at the floor for a long moment then looked back up a Brandon and nodded. Another couple came to the bar and the man went to wait on them. Brandon looked at Audrina.

"He was here," Brandon said. "He was right here."

"Yeah, he was," Audrina said, smiling.

Chapter 7

THE OASIS

Friday morning Brandon and Audrina were up early and at Denny's for breakfast. Brandon had the county map, the state map, his hand drawn map, their sequence timing record, and a legal pad. Audrina had the sphere, the calculator, and a note pad in her purse. They sipped their coffee and waited for breakfast to be served.

"It's almost seven," Brandon said. "When we finish we'll drive out to the Commercial Air Field and charter a plane, first thing. We'll fly over the area and see what's there, check out the roads, then drive out there."

"Provided a road goes to the area," Audrina added.

"If not, we'll know. We can rent the gear and hike to it." Audrina looked at Brandon, silent for a moment. He noticed her disposition and waited.

"What do we do after we find it?" she said. Brandon leaned back in his chair and blinked his eyes. Just as he started to speak, the waitress approached their table with their orders. Brandon glanced at her and smiled.

They ate in silence. When finished, Brandon pushed his plate back then took another sip of coffee.

"I don't know," he said. Audrina met his eyes; hers showed question.

"When we find it; whatever the Keepsake is in communication with; I don't know what to do about it. I guess it depends on what it is."

"You can bet it's something significant," Audrina said seriously. The Keepsake has been inert for decades and it apparently hasn't degraded its function at all.

"Let's go find it," Brandon said and picked up the ticket to pay the bill.

Brandon and Audrina drove out to the Commercial Air Field south of Roswell. Brandon steered the car into a parking lot in front of a hangar with several small planes tied down out front. They got out of the car, walked into the hangar, and looked around. Toward the back, next to the right hand wall, they saw two men in coveralls working on an aircraft engine. Brandon approached them.

"Hello," Brandon said. "Could you tell me where I could charter a plane?" The man behind the engine straightened up, a wrench in one hand and a shop towel in the other, and wiped his hands. The logo on his red and white cap read *Avery's Air Service*. He looked at Brandon, glanced at Audrina standing twenty feet away, then back to Brandon.

"You want to fly over the crash sites, huh?" he said. Brandon smiled and nodded. The mechanic nodded toward a glassed in office on the opposite side of the hangar.

"In the office, Harry Franks will take you up. Harry does that from time to time." Brandon looked toward the office, thanked the man, rejoined Audrina, and the two of them walked across the expansive hangar. They walked past a small plane, blunt nosed, and then looked back at the mechanics busy on the missing power plant.

Walking on to the office Brandon opened the door and they stepped inside. A middle-aged woman looked up from an invoice.

"Excuse me," Brandon said, "is Harry Franks around?"

"You're looking at her."

"You're Harry Franks?"

"Henrietta Franks. I didn't like Henrietta. I changed it to Harry. What can I do for you?" Brandon looked at *Harry's* steel blue eyes radiating confidence and nodded.

"I'm Brandon Stevens and this is my wife, Audrina." Harry looked at Audrina and nodded. Audrina smiled. Brandon continued: "We would like to charter a plane and fly over the crash sites."

"Two hundred dollars." Brandon presented his credit card. Harry processed it, did the numbers and handed him a pen.

"Do you take very many people over the sights?" Audrina asked.

"Two, three times a year. Nothing to see but they want to look. One fella, a writer, had me to fly the route five times. Are you a writer?" Harry said, looking from Audrina to Brandon.

"Route?" Brandon said. Harry looked up at him.

"From here to the Lincoln National Forest just this side of Capitan Peak then north to the Corona Site, then southeast to Highway 266 twenty-six miles north of Roswell, the site where they made that movie. I flew that triangle five times." Brandon and Audrina looked at each other then back to Harry.

"We're not writers," Brandon said. "My grandfather was stationed here in 1947 and out of curiosity we want to fly from the Lincoln National Forest to the Corona site and back, probably two or three times." Harry shrugged her shoulders and nodded.

"Follow me," she said then walked out of the office into the hangar then stopped abruptly. Brandon walked into her then tip toed to regain his balance. Harry glanced over her shoulder. For a second, a half smile played on her lips. She looked across the hangar at the mechanics dismantling the aircraft engine.

"Carl," she said loudly, "be back in two hours." The man behind the engine looked up then raised his hand and waved a wrench then went back to his work.

Brandon and Audrina, sitting in the back seat together, watched the grass beside the taxiway passing by the four passenger high winged aircraft. Audrina sat her purse, Keepsake inside, in the floor behind the pilot then unzipped it two inches. Brandon held a legal pad in his lap; pen in hand, to sketch access roads. Harry stopped the plane short of entering the runway. She spoke into the radio, paused, spoke again, and then entered the runway. She lined up the aircraft with the empty runway then pushed the throttle to full power. Brandon watched the ground drop away then looked to the right at Capitan Peak. At a thousand feet, Harry made a right turn then leveled off the aircraft. Speaking loudly above the din of the engine Harry said as she pointed: "That's Capitan Peak. Just this side of her we'll turn north and I'll point out the two sites to you."

"Okay," Brandon said in a strong voice, "how low can you fly?"

"Thousand feet." Audrina slipped the calculator out of a side pocket on her purse, made the calculation, and then leaned toward Brandon.

"When we are right over it the sphere will be blinking every twelve seconds." Brandon nodded then looked out the windshield. Audrina nudged him; he glanced at the purse. Audrina clicked the stopwatch and made a note of the time.

"Harry," Brandon said. "Fly directly over the Ragsdale Site then fly a straight course and fly directly over the Corona Site. Harry nodded then changed the plane's line of flight a degree or so. Minutes went by.

"We're passing over the Ragsdale Site now," Harry said. Brandon and Audrina studied the terrain then watched the slit in the purse. Audrina noted the time of the next flash then reset the stopwatch. Minutes later Audrina said:

"Two flashes at fourteen seconds; now they are getting longer." They both looked out the window and behind them.

"It's a grove of trees!" Brandon said.

"Yeah!" Audrina said. "A large grove of trees. And there's a house in the middle." They looked back at the purse and watched the flashes grow farther and farther apart. Minutes later Harry informed them they were passing over the Corona Site. Brandon leaned forward again.

"Harry, go up to three thousand feet then fly five hundred feet one side of the flight path back to the Ragsdale Site." Harry looked over her shoulder at Brandon out of the corner of her eye. Brandon smiled. Harry nodded and complied. Brandon and Audrina studied the grove of trees isolated in the desert terrain. A road came out of the trees to the east then curved south, followed a curving side-to-side route, and then connected Old Pine Lodge Road midway between the Ragsdale Site and Roswell.

Brandon instructed Harry to fly the route again. She complied. Audrina checked the numbers again. They were the same. Brandon studied the road looking for a 'land-mark' to know the road when driving Old Pine Lodge Road. He noted that the road intersected Old Pine Lodge Road and the foot of a dominate hill. He looked at Audrina and nodded. Brandon instructed the pilot that they were finished.

As Brandon drove away from the hangar and back toward Roswell, he glanced at Audrina, then back through the windshield.

"It's in those woods with that house," he said. "I wonder if somebody lives there and if they do, do they know it's there."

"Good question," Audrina said. "If they know, they've done a fantastic job of keeping it quiet." Brandon was quiet for a few moments.

"Do you suppose that it's a secret government installation? ICBM's are hidden under houses like that around the country."

"That sounds a little dramatic," Audrina said. "However, it doesn't make any sense that it would be on the flight path from the Debris Field to the Ragsdale Site and not be found." They were silent for some time as they digested the circumstances. Now that they were confronted with the unknown of having something in a grove of trees, right in the middle of the three-site triangle, transmitting to the Keepsake.

"Maybe we should find out if anybody lives there. We can drive out, look at the mailbox, get the number, then go to the Post Office and have them look at their routing map and tell us who lives there; if anybody."

"Good idea," Brandon said and headed for Old Pine Lodge Road on the other side of Roswell. Passing through the city, he turned left on Old Pine Lodge Road and drove back out into the country. He began the vigil of looking for the dominate hill indicating the desired road that led to the grove of trees concealing the secret. Soon he saw the hill and the road up ahead. He slowed then pulled off the road onto the entrance to the driveway. There a lone mailbox stood. On the side of it was printed in hand painted black lettering: *Box 121*. Brandon and Audrina looked at each other, made a U-turn, and headed for the Post Office.

They entered the Post Office, got in line behind a couple of people and waited. When their turn came, they approached the clerk and asked about getting some route information.

The clerk pointed to their right. "Go to that window in the corner; Jim can help you."

They went to the window and pushed the buzzer clearly marked *Service*. An older man appeared at the window and looked at Brandon then at Audrina. "What can I do for you?"

Audrina looked up at the clerk. "I need to know who lives at Box 121 on Old Pine Lodge Road."

"Old Pine Lodge Road is Route 3," the clerk said. "Box 121?" Audrina nodded.

"Just a minute," the clerk said and stepped away from the window. Momentarily, he reappeared with a metal box filled with index cards. He thumbed through it then lifted a card up and read it; "Elizabeth Rainwater," he said. "Actually, it's Dr. Elizabeth Rainwater. She's a doctor over here at the hospital. Last winter I got a serious case of the flu. I went to the hospital and she fixed me right up. She's in her sixties but she's the best doctor they got over there…"

"Thank you…thank you…," Audrina said making a strategic exit. Back in the car, Brandon and Audrina sat in silence for a moment.

"Okay," Brandon said, "a doctor lives there; what now?"

"Let's go out there," Audrina said. "We've come this far and the answer is there in that grove of trees. We'll knock on the door explain ourselves and…"

"I'm dying to know," Brandon said.

"Me, too."

Chapter 8

ELIZABETH RAINWATER

Audrina, holding the sphere in front of her, waited for the proximity sequence to initiate. She blinked several times when it happened, right at the spot it always did; when they drove onto Old Pine Lodge Road then drove past the Y in the road. She looked at Brandon. He was watching for it also. When it occurred, he nodded.

They were on their way to whatever was communicating with the otherworld device that Audrina held in her hand. A golf ball sized sphere that had near zero weight, metal, indestructible, and powered by some unknown energy source. A device that had been inert for half a century patiently waiting for today. This time they knew where the object on the other end of the communicating link was located.

Brandon drove on to the marker he'd picked as a locator from the air. He slowed as he descended the hill then made a right turn onto a dirt road leading off into the desert. Brandon stopped the car and put it in park. They surveyed the terrain. So far, it all looked the same.

"Well," Brandon said, "this is it. You ready?" Audrina paused a second.

"Yes." Brandon pulled the gear selector into *Drive* and began negotiating the winding dirt road.

There were ruts in places that had been driven many times. As they wound from side to side on the desert terrain, a nervous feeling crept up Brandon's spine. He glanced at Audrina; she was leaning forward holding the sphere in front of her and breathing with her mouth open. He looked back through the windshield and strained his eyes to see the tops of the trees a mile ahead. Something from another world was there. The car wandered off the road for a moment. Brandon corrected and returned it to the ruts. He glanced at Audrina again; she hadn't noticed the jostling of the car. Her attention was focused ahead. She seemed oblivious of everything around her.

The Keepsake flashed. Just as it occurred the right front tire of the car blew out explosively. Audrina screamed. Brandon jerked, then braked the car to a stop and then looked at Audrina.

"You okay?" She was gasping for breath, holding her free hand on her chest.

"Uh huh."

Brandon got out of the car, walked around the front to the passenger side and looked at the tire. It was shredded. Audrina placed the sphere on the dash and joined Brandon in front of the car. Brandon opened the trunk and got the spare, jack, and lug wrench and began the chore of jacking up the car. Audrina was standing behind him. She leaned forward and placed her hand in his shoulder.

"What?" she said.

Brandon looked around. "Huh?"

"What did you say?" Audrina repeated.

Brandon stopped and looked around again. "I didn't say anything."

"Oh, I thought you said something." Brandon removed the lug nuts, switched the tires, and then tightened them again. He began lowering the car back to the road's surface. Audrina went to the passenger door, reached in and picked up the sphere, and brought it to Brandon. He looked up at her. She handed him the Keepsake.

"Why did you bring me this?" he said. She looked confused then responded.

"Because you told me to."

"Audrina, I didn't tell you to bring me this," Brandon said holding up the sphere. Suddenly Audrina became motionless. Brandon stared at her face. He shoved the Keepsake into his pocket and grabbed her by the waist watching her eyes.

"Audrina!" She collapsed. Brandon was able to stop her fall just as her knees touched the ground. He scooped her up in his arms and placed her in the passenger seat of the car. He grabbed the shredded tire, jack, and lug wrench, threw them in the trunk and closed it. He quickly got behind the wheel then checked on Audrina. She was breathing normally but was totally unresponsive. He started the car and made a U-turn in the desert then steered back onto the road and drove as fast as he could keep control of the car on the dirt road. When he came to the highway, he accelerated toward town. Upon reaching Main Street, he turned toward downtown. In a couple of blocks, he saw a police officer stopped at a convenience store. He'd come out of the store on his way to his car. Brandon hurriedly steered the car into the parking lot and over to the officer.

"My wife collapsed! Where's the hospital!" The officer glanced at Audrina then back to Brandon.

"Follow me," the officer said then got behind the wheel of his cruiser, turned on the lights, then entered the traffic. Brandon saw him talking into his radio. Moments later, they pulled into the hospital entrance and into the bay of the emergency room. Brandon jumped out of the car, hurried around to the passenger side and picked up Audrina. Two orderlies came out the door of the emergency room with a gurney. Brandon put Audrina on it. They hurriedly took her into the emergency room and on to an examining room. Moments later a doctor and a nurse entered the room as the orderlies exited. He quickly checked Audrina's respiratory function, looked in her mouth, then her eyes with a pencil light. He placed his stethoscope on Audrina's chest and listened for a moment then looked up at Brandon.

"Her pulse, breathing, and responses all seem okay. What happened?" Brandon explained the changing of the tire and her collapse for no apparent reason.

"Perhaps she got too hot,"

"No," Brandon countered; "we were driving on a dirt road in an air conditioned car."

"Any family history of unexplained fainting spells?"

"No." Bandon persisted. "None." Audrina began to stir then opened her eyes. Brandon quickly grabbed her hand and called her name. She sat up and looked at him.

"What happened?" she said.

"Are you okay?" Brandon said.

"Of course I am; why wouldn't I be?" Audrina looked around the room. "Where are we?"

"At the hospital. You collapsed out on that road to Doctor Rainwater's house." When the young doctor in attendance heard Brandon's explanation, he leaned toward his nurse. "Go get Doctor Rainwater." The nurse hurried out the door.

Doctor Elizabeth Rainwater pushed the curtain aside and entered the examining room. The young doctor and nurse left. Brandon was talking with Audrina. He turned around to greet the doctor.

"You wanted to see me?" she said. Brandon glanced at Audrina. She nodded. Brandon nodded in agreement.

"Yes, Ms. Rainwater. Is there some place where we could talk?" Elizabeth searched Brandon and Audrina's faces, paused a moment, then nodded.

"My office. Follow me."

"Ms. Rainwater, this might be a little difficult to explain. A special device led us to your house..."

Elizabeth straightened up in her chair. "Did you arrive here in Roswell Wednesday just before noon?"

Brandon and Audrina looked at each other. "Yes, yes we did."

"Oh my God!" Elizabeth said, "You have the Initiator!"

Brandon and Audrina looked at each other for a moment then Brandon reached into his pocket, pulled out the Keepsake, and held it up. "This?"

Elizabeth's eyes widened. She reached and took the sphere and stared at it. "Where did you find it?"

Audrina turned to Brandon. "Go get the letter for Ms. Rainwater."

Brandon stood. "Excuse me, I want to go to our car and get something that will explain what we are doing here."

Elizabeth nodded. Brandon left the office. Elizabeth turned to Audrina.

"You fainted in the desert on the road to my house?" Audrina nodded.

"Did you hear a voice talking to you before you fainted?"

"Ah, Yes!" Audrina said. "I thought it was my husband talking to me." Brandon stepped through the door into the office with the letter in his hand. He explained where and how he got the letter then handed it to Elizabeth. She unfolded it and read it, glanced up at Brandon and Audrina, then read it again. "We knew the Initiator was back in the area. The Locator started flashing just before noon

Wednesday. It indicated that this would come close then go farther away, then close again, then out of range."

"Locator? What's the Locator?" Brandon said. Elizabeth paused and leaned back in her chair as if collecting herself. After a few moments she looked at Brandon and Audrina.

"I don't know any other way to tell you this except straight out. One of the crewmembers of the spaceship that crashed in the Lincoln National Forest survived and is living at my house."

Brandon and Audrina stared at Elizabeth for a moment. "Oh, my God!" Brandon said.

Audrina leaned forward. "Is it there, now?!"

"It's a he, and yes, he's there, now. His name is Orion. My father gave him that name when he found out where he's from; the Orion star cluster."

"I'm sorry," Audrina said. Elizabeth smiled.

"Don't worry about it. The first time I saw him, when I was twelve, that's what I said. What is it? That was fifty years ago. We, my parents and I, were camping in the Lincoln National Forest on that July 4 weekend when his ship came down and crashed. We were a quarter of a mile from where it hit. We heard the storm and the big explosion north of us. We thought it was lightening hitting the ground or a tree or something. Just before daylight, while sleeping in our tent, Orion, hiding in the trees, approached our campsite and spoke to my father; ah, to his mind. Dad woke up, raised up on one elbow, looked out the tent door, and saw Orion. He was standing there trembling. Dad said that at first he thought he was dreaming. But, Orion spoke again. He was saying, *"Help me."* He was holding one arm that was limp, with the other.

"Dad woke us and told us about him and that he was going to help him. At the time, we didn't know where he came from. I thought he was neat. It took my mother a while to calm down; but she did. We took him home with us. That day, Dad, being a doctor, was called to the base in Roswell, sworn to secrecy, and then asked to do autopsies on the bodies they found in the crashed ships. That's when Dad fully understood where Orion came from.

"He decided to harbor Orion because of that experience at the base. He knew what might happen to Orion because of the fear everyone had of the aliens that were there. Dad said one of aliens at the base was still alive when he got there but was hurt pretty bad. He and another doctor patched it up and the military spirited it away somewhere. He never knew where and never heard anything about it again.

"Orion became a member of our family. He has spent the last fifty years learning about Earth from radio and TV.

"He's the one that spoke to you. They can do that; mental projection of thought. It can cause disorientation or fainting as you experienced, however, you get used to it. Most of the time I speak aloud when I answer him. Would you like to meet him?" Elizabeth got to her feet. Brandon and Audrina stood.

"Yes!" Audrina said. Elizabeth picked up the phone, dialed, and then announced that she was leaving for the day. She hung it up, then handed the Keepsake to Audrina.

"He's going to want this. He has one just like it. He said it was the wrong one. It is set for one of the other student's safety device. Apparently, the Initiators got mixed up when they crashed their spaceship. The one you have activated the proximity function on his Locator; so, it's the right one. He's waited a long time for it."

Elizabeth, driving slowly along the dirt road leading to her home, slowed her car to a stop just before reaching the point of the incident with Audrina's collapse. Brandon and Audrina quickly got out of their car and hurried to her open door. Elizabeth looked one to the other.

"I wanted to warn you. Orion will greet you again about the top of that rise," she said, pointing toward the grove of trees ahead. "When he speaks to you, just relax and let your mind work. Actually, it's neat. You can talk to people farther from you without shouting." She smiled then closed the car door again and eased the machine forward. Brandon and Audrina quickly returned to their car and followed. Moments later:

"Hello."
Audrina sat up in the seat and took a couple of deep breaths.

Brandon looked at her: "Audr…"

Audrina held up her hand and calmed her breathing then spoke out loud: "Hello, my name is Audrina."

"Dr. Compton C. Rainwater, my friend, gave me the name, Orion. Elizabeth said you were okay."

"Yes," Audrina said and visibly nodded.

"Bring me the Initiator."

"Yes, okay." Audrina looked at Brandon and smiled.

"That is spooky," Brandon said and then resumed following Elizabeth.

Elizabeth entered the grove of trees surrounding the older two-story house and followed the winding road up into the yard. Brandon followed and pulled their car up beside hers. Elizabeth opened her door, got out, and stood. Movement in a window on the second floor caught Audrina's eye. She glanced upward to see the curtains fall back together. She looked at Brandon; he had seen it too.

"Do you realize what's about to happen?"

"Are we dreaming?" Brandon said, staring at the upstairs window.

"I've pinched myself three times," Audrina said.

Brandon and Audrina, standing on either side of Elizabeth, watched the front door of the older home open slowly. Their eyes fell on a

Creature about three feet tall, its shoulder even with the doorknob. His head, as wide as his shoulders with dominate eyes about three inches across, was mounted on a neck less than three inches in diameter. His arms extended down to halfway between the hip and the knee.

He was clothed in a single piece coverall-type suit, silvery in color, with a donut shaped device around his waist. His large eyes went from Brandon to Audrina then to the Keepsake. A small light on his waist-worn device was flashing in unison with the sphere. His skin was gray with a rugged appearing texture. Brandon looked for and found three fingers. The creature looked uncannily like the rendition on the hospital bed displayed at the UFO Museum in Roswell. Elizabeth nodded toward Orion then glanced from Audrina to Brandon.

"You two okay?" Brandon and Audrina paused a moment then nodded in unison. Orion projected to both Brandon and Audrina: *Hello.* Audrina smiled and replied. Brandon caught his breath and touched his head.

"You okay?" Audrina asked.

Brandon took another breath and exhaled. "Yeah. I didn't know you could feel words." Brandon looked at Orion for a moment. "Where are you from?" Orion looked up at Brandon.

"Your Dr. Rainwater gave me a name; the name of my home. On your star charts, it's called the Orion star cluster. My planet circles the middle star of Orion's Belt. Your name of that star is Alnilam."

"That's over a thousand lightyears away. How long did it take you to get...?"

"Wait, Brandon," Audrina interrupted. She handed Orion the Keepsake and the three of them entered the living room and closed the door. It was flashing so fast it was virtually a constant pinkish glow. Orion paused a moment then turned to Elizabeth.

"Elizabeth, when I insert this Initiator into my Locator device it will transmit a location signal to my people. They will come for me. I don't know when they will arrive; I don't know how close they are." Elizabeth nodded.

Orion removed the inert Initiator and inserted the Keepsake into the donut shaped device circling his waist. The device glowed a pinkish light for several seconds then went dark. Orion removed the Keepsake and returned it to Audrina then reinserted the original. Brandon pointed at the sphere in Orion's device.

"That one doesn't work, huh?"

Orion projected the answer: *"It's for a device that was worn by one of the other students."* Orion then turned toward Elizabeth and nodded. Elizabeth looked at Orion and smiled then turned to Brandon.

"There's something else about that thing he's wearing around his waist. He can use it to disappear."

"What?" Brandon said.

"Orion can become invisible anytime. It has made it possible to hide him all these years. When someone accidently saw him, he immediately sensed it, activated that device, and just winked out. After that it was fairly easy to talk the *witness* out of really seeing him." Elizabeth smiled disarmingly.

"A cloaking device?!" Brandon said. Elizabeth turned to Orion and nodded.

Orion touched a button on the front of the donut shaped appliance. His body became transparent then winked out. Audrina gasped. Brandon reached forward with his hand. It disappeared. He jerked it back then wiggled his fingers and made a fist a couple of times. No ill effects. Again, he reached into the generated field and touched an invisible shoulder. Orion was still there. Momentarily Orion reappeared then looked up a Brandon.

"I don't believe it!" Brandon said enthusiastically, "How does it work?"

Orion put both of his hands on the device around his waist. *"This device generates a quantum field in the fabric of space and the light rays follow the projected lines around me. Our ships have the same capability."*

Brandon's jaw dropped. "Have you been coming to Earth and checking us out."

Orion looked up at Brandon again then cocked his head to the side. *"No. We've just begun exploring this part of the galaxy. Your discovery of nuclear fission brought us directly to your planet."*

Elizabeth had been quiet for some time. Orion sensed her demeanor of sadness. He spoke quietly to her in her mind. She looked up then took Orion in her arms for a moment. He circled her with his long arms. Orion spoke again to all three minds:

"Thank you, Elizabeth Rainwater, for fifty years of a safe harbor and thanks to your father for taking me in and saving my life here on planet Earth. I know a lot about you. I have much to report."

"You know what I am thinking, don't you," Elizabeth said.

"Yes," Orion projected. Brandon and Audrina looked at each other with question on their faces. Elizabeth looked up at them.

"You take Orion with you until his people come for him. I'm getting older and you two are still young and fresh. He needs someone to watch out for him until the day he's reunited with his own." Brandon and Audrina looked at each other for a moment and nodded in unison.

"We would like that," Audrina said.

Elizabeth stepped into her home office, returned with her business card, and handed it to Audrina. "Call me from time to time, especially the day he's picked up."

Audrina nodded.

Chapter 9

THE CODER

Azell Harriman adjusted his thick glasses, switched hands with the heavy briefcase, and then knocked on the office door of Agent Charles Stockton deep inside the Jet Propulsion Laboratories. The door opened and a tall thin woman with close-cropped hair beckoned for the aged code specialist to enter. He was escorted to the agent's private office. He entered the spacious room and took a seat indicated by a wave of the agent's hand. He adjusted the nod of his head to focus through his, once again, new prescription of no-line bifocals Stockton looked up, blinked several times, closed a folder, and laced his fingers together.

"Well, Azell, I understand that you have something to show me; something that you could not courier here; something you had to deliver personally." Azell, as if on cue, leaned forward, opened his briefcase, pulled out a file jacket, and then got to his feet. He looked at Stockton again, adjusted the nod, and then began to deliver a report that he'd waited fifty years to give.

"At first I thought it was just a power surge that fried the electronics in the IG519-A satellite," he said. "But," he indicated the file jacket, "as it turns out; it's more—much more."

"What?" Stockton said, interested. Azell walked across the office, turned an adjusted the nod again, then gestured with his hand.

"Are you familiar with the Missing Midget Summary presented to this office in late 1947?" Stockton frowned at the unexpected inquiry. "I know it was before your time...," Azell added.

"I read it," Stockton interrupted. "Two saucers crashed, a total of ten seats, only nine aliens were found, where's the other one?"

"Ah, you read it," Azell said. "It is well that you did...well that you did." Azell paused, still looking at the agent, with his head cocked back and his mouth open.

CIA Agent Charles Manly Stockton began to get irritated with constantly looking up the nose holes of the older code specialist. He didn't like him. He never did. The only thing keeping the obnoxious little seventy-one-year old here was his uncanny ability to decipher signals. The old fart knew it and chose to be deliberately irritating. He'd get rid of him as soon as there was a window of opportunity. Or, maybe he would die. Stockton leaned back in his chair.

"I can tell you where the Missing Midget is. He died on the way here and they committed his body to *deep space*. The military would have found him if he'd been on that ship that crashed in those trees. They sifted that area for twenty years." Azell smiled, and then opened the file jacket. He pulled out a report consisting of several pages of technical information, and then a page typed in plain language.

"That power surge that destroyed the satellite was a very powerful transmission beamed toward the Orion Star Cluster." Azell gestured with the report as he spoke.

"Beamed from where?" Stockton said.

"Roswell, New Mexico." Stockton forgot about the nose holes. He unlaced his fingers, laid his hands flat on the desk and stared at the report in the expert's hand.

"Now," Azell continued, "I took the ten second signal, isolated it, then started slowing it down. When I got it slow enough, what it really was, jumped out." Stockton straightened up in his chair.

"What was it?" he said, leaning forward. Azell stepped over to his desk and laid the plain typed paper in front of him.

"Coordinates," he said. "A set of four coordinates."

"Coordinates!" Stockton said and grabbed the sheet of paper and scanned it.

It read:

.611138791125 000000000000 .217680000004

3

33 23 46

"Our Missing Midget sent a message home," Azell said. *"Come and get me."* Stockton looked at the typed page again.

"Is this the whole message?" Azell nodded.

"How did you get that from this," Stockton said pointing at the coordinates. He knew the old man was right. Hell, he always was.

"On the first set of coordinates," Azell began, "the first set of numbers is how far the Solar System is from the Galactic Core, counting the distance from the Galactic Core to the edge of the Galaxy, as one. It checks out. The second set of numbers is the location of the Solar System relative to the Galactic Plane. It checks out. The third set—this took me a couple of hours, is...

"Wow," Stockton interjected. Azell glanced at the agent for a moment then chose to ignore it.

"...is how far the Solar System is off a line drawn from the Galactic Core through the Orion Star Cluster to the edge of the Galaxy. It checks out." Azell looked at Stockton. The agent's eyes still showed question.

"The set of three groups of numbers is how to get to the Solar System from Orion," Azell concluded. Stockton looked back at the list.

"And the second entry is...." Stockton looked up at Azell; they said it together, "the third planet."

"The other two entries are Earth coordinates," Azell finished.

"Where?!" Stockton said awkwardly.

"Roswell, New Mexico." Stockton jumped up from his desk and walked rapidly around it toward the door. He abruptly stopped in the middle of the room and turned. He didn't know where he was going. He quickly began studying the page again. He looked up at Azell.

"When? Do you know when *they* will be here?" Azell shook his head.

"The message did not conclude," Azell offered. "Transmissions usually conclude with "*Over*," signing off, awaiting your reply, etc.; there was nothing as if the transmitter was deliberately left open but only for incoming. I'm not sure what to make of it. My educated guess is the transmitter continually updates itself on his location so he can move around to avoid being discovered. Then the transmitter will update his rescuer when the ship communicates with it.

"You'll be able to pick up that transmission?"

"Yes, and I will be able to tell you where the signal came from. However, there's no way to know how much time you have to get there. Here's another thing," Azell continued: "The Orion Star Cluster is over a thousand lightyears away from Earth. Unless their communications are different from ours, his message will not arrive there for over a thousand years. It seems to me that there would be no point in sending it. Therefore, I believe they can communicate in the Quantum World where any distance is instant. Or, Agent Stockton, they have a mother ship nearby; out at the edge of the Solar System or perhaps at the Lagrange Point. At any rate our Missing Midget is still in Roswell; at least he was yesterday afternoon when this message was transmitted."

Stockton hurried back behind his desk, sat down in his chair and grabbed the phone then looked up at the aging code specialist.

"Thank you, Azell. Not a word..."

"Of course not," Azell interrupted then picked up his briefcase and stepped to the door, opened it, then stopped and turned toward Stockton. The agent put the phone back on the cradle without dialing then raised his eyebrows.

"What's our Missing Midget been doing the past fifty years?" Azell said, holding the agent's eyes for a moment, then went out the door and closed it.

Agent Stockton picked up the phone.

Chapter 10

HOUSTON

Brandon and Audrina, with their *charge*, left Elizabeth Rainwater in the late afternoon, planning a fourteen-hour drive with only brief stops for fuel and service station sandwiches, to finally pull into their garage in rural Houston. They plotted a course of heading south through Carlsbad and on to Interstate 10, and then follow it across the bottom of the country to Houston. Orion, sitting in the back seat, would *wink out* while passing through cities, towns, and oases on their route.

The Sun was just pushing away the darkness in the early morning sky when they arrived. Exhausted, they showed Orion to the guest room, pointed out the TV, and then informed him that they must rest. He nodded and turned on the TV and settled down in front of it.

Brandon and Audrina finished a bacon and egg breakfast at 11:00 a.m. Orion ate a piece of bread. Brandon looked at Audrina.

"Dad and Mom, especially Mom, have a right to know about the secret segment of Grandpa's life. Grandpa kept it quiet because of orders by the military. But, I believe, considering what we found because of his gift to me, he would want his daughter to know. His experience in the military did affect his life. Also, his daughter faithfully keeping her promise to him turned out to be very significant. I'm going to call Dad and Mom and ask them to come down this afternoon and stay overnight so they can meet Orion."

"I agree," Audrina said. "Your mother was magnificent with that promise. You'd better prepare them to meet Orion; let them read the letter, show the Keepsake and discuss it. What is your father's position toward the possibility of extraterrestrials?"

"Average, I guess. We've never discussed the subject in detail." Brandon picked up the phone, called his parents, and spent some time explaining that he and Audrina were back home early because of what Grandpa left him. It was so unusual that he wanted them to drive down to Houston for a visit so he could show them the *gift*. His mother, intrigued, agreed. They would leave in about an hour and arrive around 6:00 p.m.

Brandon and Audrina spent the afternoon communicating to Orion the details of the adventure they had experienced in past days that lead up to this moment. Their concern was that Orion might communicate with Ray and Kathleen without encountering difficulty. There was much to consider, especially if Orion's rescue proved to be a long drawn out affair. They wondered what the wisdom was here. In a better world, they would be able to call the NASA Administrator and make an appointment to introduce him to Orion. Then he would make the arrangements to introduce Orion to the President and hence to America and on to planet Earth. Then have, on TV for the benefit of all, the meeting of all time. But, Earth was not ready for that simple approach. It wasn't ready in 1938 during the Orson Wells radio show. The listening audience at the time, most beginning to listen after the fictional drama about aliens had started, believed it was real and panic spread rapidly throughout the area. There was an even worse reaction in the 1947 Roswell Incident. And, save for a group of dedicated scientists, Earth is not ready now. Brandon and Audrina had some serious thinking to do and a prudent action to take, or perhaps, not take.

6:15 p.m. - Rural Houston

"Okay," Kathleen said, sitting at the dining room table with Ray, Brandon, and Audrina, "what did Dad give you?" Brandon, holding this grandfather's letter in his hand, looked up at his mother.

"A fantastic adventure and an answer to a very big question. Mom, Dad, did Grandpa ever mention aliens or extraterrestrials to you?" Ray and Kathleen looked at each other then back to Brandon. Ray responded:

"Ah, he might have mentioned sometime through the years. You know, there has been lots of movies and books about the subject. I don't recall any specific conversation on the matter. Why?" Brandon's mother looked from Ray's face to Brandon.

"When we opened the bank box in Wichita Falls there was a blue velvet draw string pouch inside. In the pouch was this." Brandon handed his mother the Keepsake. She looked it over, noted its lack of weight then handed it to Ray. For a moment, they both looked up at Brandon. He handed them the letter. "This was in the pouch with it." They read the letter together then Kathleen took it and read it again.

"Oh, my God!" She said looking from face to face. "The Roswell Crash; he was involved with the Roswell Crash!"

"There's more," Brandon said, "a lot more. When Audrina and I read that letter and saw the sphere we decided to go to Roswell and see what we could find out about it. When we got close to the crash sites," Brandon picked up the Keepsake, "This started flashing."

"Flashing?" Ray said.

Brandon nodded. "It turned out that this is a proximity device. You can locate whatever is transmitting to it by measuring how far apart the flashes are. We drove site to site and did some measuring and discovered that what it was transmitting to was at a house in a grove of trees out in the desert near Roswell." Ray and Kathleen were listening intently. Brandon continued: "We got the number off the mailbox, went to the post office, and discovered that a doctor lived in the house. A doctor Elizabeth Rainwater." Brandon glanced at Audrina and decided to skip the episode with Audrina's collapse and visit to the hospital.

Brandon continued: "We went to the hospital, found her, and told her about the Keepsake leading us to her house. At that point she told us a most unusual and fantastic story; a true story.

This Keepsake was electronically connected to an alien device that was on the spaceship that crashed at Roswell in 1947. Elizabeth, twelve years old at the time, and her parents; Dr. Compton Rainwater and his wife, were camping about a quarter mile away from where the ship crashed that night. One of the aliens that was on that ship survived the crash. He was injured but was able to get out of the ship and hide in the forest. The alien made its way through the woods to the tent where the Rainwater's were camping, approached them, and asked for help with its injuries. Dr. Rainwater exercised compassion and rendered aid to the *Creature*. They took it home with them to heal.

"The following day Compton Rainwater was called to the base at Roswell Army Air Field to do autopsies on the aliens that were killed in the crash. Seeing the Army's reaction, he decided to conceal the injured one at his house."

"Is it still alive, I mean, still living?!" Kathleen said.

"Yes," Brandon said. "It's a he, and his wounds healed and he was okay. Now, Mom,

Dad, brace yourselves. Elizabeth Rainwater is in her sixties and she asked us to bring Orion, that's his name, with us and watch out for him until his people get here to take him home. We agreed and...we did." Kathleen and Ray stared at Brandon for a long moment then looked over at Audrina then back to Brandon.

"Where is he?" Kathleen asked.

Brandon paused a moment then turned toward the guest room door. "Orion."

Ray and Kathleen's eyes went to the door. It slowly opened. Orion stepped out of the doorway and into the room. Kathleen took a breath then her hand went over her mouth.

Ray caught his breath. "Son-of-a-gun!"

Brandon spoke up: "Orion can speak directly to you mind. Just relax and let the thoughts in. Brandon nodded to Orion. He spoke to both Ray and Kathleen.

"*Bandon told me about your father. I'm glad to meet you.*" Kathleen, breathing heavily, nodded.

As the evening wore on communications with Orion became, more or less, conversational. If you didn't look to see if his mouth was moving it seemed relatively normal. Orion, on his second day as a houseguest of Brandon and Audrina spoke to them dually.

"*I have watched your television. I have learned many of things about you, your planet, and your culture. You are a planet of divided peoples. You war with each other. For this reason, you have developed monitoring machines. Those machines probably picked up my transmission to my people. What do you think they will do?"* Brandon and Audrina looked at each other.

"I hadn't thought about that," Brandon said. "If they picked up the signal, and you can bet they did, they will send a team to Roswell to find you."

"Elizabeth needs to be warned," Audrina said and stepped over to the phone. She opened her purse and pulled out Elizabeth's card then dialed the number for her home. Elizabeth's voice seemed strong and upbeat.

"Dr. Rainwater," came from the phone. Audrina sat down in her chair.

"Elizabeth, this is Audrina."

"Well, Hello, how's my alien?" Audrina laughed.

"He's fine. We introduced him to Brandon's parents yesterday; he was a hit."

"I'll bet he was."

"Elizabeth," Audrina began, "we wanted to warn you. Orion said that his transmission to his people was more than likely picked up by the nations monitoring equipment. NORAD, or JPL, or maybe other listeners of the sky. Brandon thinks they may send someone to Roswell to see if they can find something. They may be knocking on your door."

"Don't worry about it," Elizabeth said, "I've got lots of practice." Through the years, on several occasions, people have actually seen Orion. He would quickly blink out. Most of the time the *witness* simply would shake his or her head and

107

dismiss it. A few times it took the *victim* a while to declare it a hallucination, with my help, of course."

Audrina and Elizabeth visited on the phone for some time. Audrina gave Elizabeth an open invitation to come and visit Orion anytime. Perhaps he would be leaving soon and Elizabeth might wish to say goodbye again. Elizabeth indicated she just might do that.

Brandon, Audrina, Ray, Kathleen, and Orion, sitting at an 8:00 a.m. breakfast, began discussions on a very awkward development. A houseguest from the Alnilam Solar System.

"Okay," Brandon said, "we are sitting on a powder keg here." Audrina looked up at Brandon then at Orion. He was eating from a box of Post Toasties, one at a time.

"What do we do now?" Brandon added.

Audrina responded. "If we are going to protect Orion until the arrival of his people we are going to have to go about business as usual so nobody will suspect he's here."

"That's what you should do," Kathleen said.

Brandon and Audrina walked Ray and Kathleen to their car. Kathleen looked up at Brandon.

"Let us know when his people get here and he's actually safely with them.

Brandon nodded. "I will, Mom."

Chapter 11

AGENT STOCKTON

Agent Charles Stockton stepped off the airliner in Albuquerque, New Mexico. Theron Wilson, black, too young to be smart, too smart to be young, an agent with the best of both worlds, met him; shook hands, then indicated the direction to the commuter plane to transfer them to Roswell.

"I read the Missing Midget Summary," Wilson said, "and Azell's report. You really believe that one of the aliens has been hanging around Roswell for fifty years?"

"Azell has never been wrong."

"There's a first time for..."

"In a way I hope he's wrong. However, Agent Wilson, are you prepared to ignore his report?"

"No."

When Stockton and Wilson approached the commuter plane, a suited figure exited a private jet sitting nearby with its engines running and walked to intercept the path of the two agents. They paused in a defensive posture. The figure held up an open palm while his other went inside his suit coat pocket and came out with his identification. He was the CIA's Regional Director. He instructed the two agents to enter the private jet. They complied. The plane immediately taxied out for takeoff.

"Agents Stockton and Wilson," the Director read from his memo. They both nodded. "I'm Regional Director Elliot Scanlon."

Agent Wilson asked, "Where are we going, Sir?"

"Houston."

The private jet lined up on a Houston runway and continued on to touchdown then taxied up to a car waiting at the parking area. Scanlon escorted Stockton and Wilson to it. They entered and the driver drove out of the airport and headed southwest out of Houston.

"Gentlemen," Elliot Scanlon said. "You know of EBE?"

Stockton and Wilson's eyes went to the director. "Yeah," Stockton said, "he's one of the aliens that crashed in Roswell in 1947 and survived the crash but finally died in 1952."

"I heard his body is pickled somewhere," Agent Theron Wilson added.

Scanlon smiled and paused for a few moments, then shook his head.

Stockton's eyes widened. "He's still alive!"

Scanlon nodded. "In '52, he tried to escape. In his holding area, back then, they devised a trap, a net over the whole room attached to a heavy ring that could be dropped over him. That was done because they discovered that a device he was wearing around his waist had the capability of cloaking him; making him invisible at the push of a button. The device could not be removed without killing him. So, they rigged the capture net. On one of the daily routine entrances with his food, he disappeared. They triggered the trap. It got him. When it fell, it shattered one of his arms and, at the same time, it damaged the device around his waist. At least he hasn't *winked out* since. They had to remove one of his arms—the right one.

"The conspiracy theorists and UFO buffs were calling so much attention to him that people in high places began to put pressure on for a congressional investigation. The CIA decided to let it out that he did die that year. It worked. Things began to settle down. We quietly constructed him a new home here in South Texas."

"Oh, my God!" Stockton said, "EBE is still alive! Where is he?"

Scanlon smiled again. "You are about to meet him."

"Sir," Theron Wilson said, 'how did this Creature get the name EBE?"

Scanlon looked at the young agent. "According to my superiors when I was first introduced to the alien, a young, brilliant, Entomologist, Dana Caray was contacted and taken to meet the alien and was asked to examine him and determine exactly what he was. Caray must be crowding eighty now. Anyway, he said the Creature was a combination of insectoid, reptilian, and hominid. He gave him the name EBE; Extraterrestrial Biological Entity. This Caray believes that the *Creature* was genetically engineered for space travel."

An hour out of Houston the driver turned onto a blacktop road, proceeded several hundred yards to a gate of a fenced in area, and stopped beside a pedestal with a key pad on it. The gate and fence were some ten feet high enclosing a farming area. Inside the agents saw a tractor plowing in a field of some type of green crop. A large sign on the gate read: GMO TESTING AREA – KEEP OUT.

The driver typed in a code; the gate slowly rolled along its track to full open. He drove through it; it promptly closed. He turned to the right and drove a quarter of a mile then turned left and drove into a large open air shed and stopped the car. Scanlon got out, motioned for his fellow agents to follow, and walked into a large equipment shed.

Parked all around were several tractors and farming implements. Farther on there was a tool room against the back wall. Next to it, there was a glassed in sunroom. Beyond that, there were several agricultural offices with a staff sitting at individual desks apparently busy with their research efforts.

Scanlon approached the tool room, opened its door, escorted Stockton and Wilson inside, and closed it. He opened a panel on the wall and pushed a button. The floor of the room started downward in an elevator style movement.

"Sir," Agent Wilson said, "I saw a sunroom up there beside the tool shed."

"That's for EBE. Dana Caray, the Entomologist that named EBE, was with a University here in Houston and was considered the nation's foremost authority in his field at twenty-eight years old. The guy was a genius. He clued us in on the fact that the *Creature* has to have sunlight ever so often or his health will gradually go bad and we would lose him. He would have died and we would not have known why. We had that sunroom built next to the tool room and offices. He's taken up there—daily—for a couple of hours."

Some hundred feet or so down the shaft the elevator stopped. Scanlon opened the door again and the three agents stepped out of the elevator into an underground laboratory. There were several people, dressed in white lab type coats, working in small offices. Scanlon walked the length of the room and opened another door, then another.

Stepping through the last door, they saw him. On the right, a stainless steel mesh type wire, floor to ceiling wall to wall, cordoned off half the room. Inside was a Creature about three feet tall with a proportionately large head and a frail body. It was gray skinned and had very large eyes. Its right arm, from just above the elbow down, was missing. The remaining portion of the arm appeared to be just a skin covered bone extending from the shoulder downward about ten inches.

"Gentlemen," Scanlon said, "meet EBE." The two agent's eyes went back to the small *Creature*.

EBE, sitting on a small bed, focused on Stockton's mind for a moment, got to his feet, then approached the wire and looked up at him.

"*They've come for me*?" Stockton's hands went to the sides of his head; he took two steps backward, breathing heavily. EBE hurried back to his bed and sat down. The Director grabbed Stockton by the shoulders and steadied him, then looked from him to EBE then back to Stockton's face.

"What happened!?" he said loudly. Agent Stockton slowly regained his self-control. "He asked me if his people have come for him!"

Back in Roswell, New Mexico

The Director's private jet touched down at the Roswell Airport. He addressed Stockton and Wilson:

"Find the *Creature* that sent the message Azell intercepted." The Director's aircraft again took to the skies.

They had to start somewhere. It seems that an alien, a very noticeable, easy to spot, very

114

different, *Creature* has managed to hide himself in Roswell for half a century. He must have had help.

They would visit all the sites involved in the incident and the museum in Roswell. Maybe something would turn up. They possessed the knowledge that one of the aliens was here two days ago. It could be here right now as far as they knew. Who would likely help an alien, hide him, and feed him? Fifty years is a long time to stay out of sight.

Stockton and his cohort rented a car, drove into Roswell, and pulled up in front of the lobby of the Best Western Motel. The agents requested a room isolated as possible for an indefinite stay. They were booked into a room in the back of facility. Bag and baggage inside they began to plan the hunt.

Chapter 12

THE ENTOMOLOGIST

Monday morning Brandon drove through Houston to the campus of the University of Texas and parked in front of the Administration Building. He entered the offices and approached an older lady occupying one of several desks half mooned around the reception area. She looked up and smiled. Brandon readied his story.

"I'm Brandon Stevens.   I graduated University of Texas at Arlington. I'm looking at some research in a certain field of study. I need to talk to the University's foremost Entomologist.

"You missed him by four years. He retired in '94. However, he still grants interviews and/or sessions from time to time. I could call him and see if he will see you and when. What subject do you want to discuss with Professor Caray?"

Brandon paused a moment, made a decision, then continued in an even tone: "Tell him it's about one of the subjects he examined years ago; tell him it's about EBE."

"EBE? What's that?"

"It's a nickname he picked a long time ago. He'll know what it means." The lady smiled and picked up the phone and dialed.

"Professor Caray, this is Dolores at the University. Sir, there's a graduate student here that would like to talk to you about EBE; whatever that is." She sat motionless for a moment. "Professor?" Momentarily she nodded and hung up the phone. Then looked up at Brandon.

"He said you could come to his house right now. That's very unusual."

Brandon smiled and nodded. "Hey, I'm lucky. How do I get to his house?"

The lady smiled and nodded then opened her pencil drawer and handed Brandon the professor's card.

Brandon drove straight to the professor's home to look at the area. It was one of Houston's nicer inter-loop neighborhoods. The houses were about a block apart and recessed off the street some hundred yards or so.

"Looks like this guy did well," Brandon muttered, then drove home. He explained the morning so far to Audrina. They made the decision to take Orion and go visit the professor. Brandon wanted to know more about Orion. They explained Brandon's motive to Orion.

Orion knew of EBE and his fate from the many television presentations over the years. EBE had lost his life in captivity. This professor had seen him and examined him. It was a connection of sorts. Orion was glad for an opportunity to go and see him.

Brandon picked up his briefcase and took it with them, placing it in the back seat with Orion to have an excuse to open the back door of the car if, for some reason, he was being observed while at the professor's home. Orion would be cloaked.

"Brandon drove up the long driveway of Professor Dana Caray's home and stopped the car. He knocked on the door of the house and waited. Momentarily a middle aged lady opened it. "May I help you?"

"Yes, I'm Brandon Stevens, I'm here to see the professor."

"What's this about?"

"The professor is expecting me. I'm here to talk about EBE."

"Oh, yes, Mr. Stevens, the professor's in his study."

"Let me get my wife," Brandon said. The lady nodded and smiled. Brandon stepped out to the car and opened the door for Audrina, then opened the back door and picked up his briefcase and stepped back for a moment. Orion exited the car and stepped close to Audrina. With Brandon leading, they entered the house and were escorted into the professor's study. The professor's caregiver stepped out of the study and closed the doors. Professor Caray looked up from his diary, turned and studied Brandon's face for a moment, then glanced at Audrina.

"How did you know it was me?"

"I took a guess, Professor, an educated guess based on the remoteness of the event, your age, and, most of all, *foremost authority on*

Entomology. Those three things pointed to you. I was right."

The professor nodded and smiled. Brandon spoke up: "Professor, I want to tell you a story, a true story, and then I want your permission to show you something very significant.

The professor gestured with his hand: *You have the floor.*

Brandon began the story with his grandfather's find in '47 and continued with his narrative until he drove up the professor's driveway this day. When finished he looked at the professor. "May I have your permission to introduce you to another survivor of the Roswell crash?" The professor sat straight up in his chair.

"Yes, you may."

Brandon turned. "Orion."

Orion became visible standing at the end of the professor's desk. A big smile spread across Professor Caray's face. "EBE could do that!"

"Too bad he died," Brandon said. The professor looked from Orion to Brandon.

"Yeah, it was a sad day for me when I heard about it. Back in '47 I spent a couple of weeks with him. He was underground at Andrews Airforce Base then. They were desperately trying to find out who he was, where he came from, and what he was. They were afraid that the public would panic if they knew about him, like people did during the 1938 radio show. Only, this time, with a real live alien, they were afraid of a much worse nationwide reaction."

Professor, you examined EBE and, I understand, determined his basic makeup, right?"

"Yes, he was a genetic mix of insectoid, reptilian, and hominid. They're the best physical traits for space travel. They figured out how to get the chromosome issue to work without a perfect match. It's brilliant." The professor studied Orion's countenance again then turned to Brandon.

"Mr. Stevens, what are you going to do with Orion?"

"His people are coming for him."

"Oh, when?"

"He doesn't know how long it will be. He sent the message out last Friday. It could be a while."

"If he sent out a transmission, they are now looking for him. They are very good at that; scary good at it. If you need any help shielding him, I will help. Any time you need too, you can drop him off here for a while. I'll talk to my caregiver so he won't give her a heart attack." Brandon and Audrina smiled with the professor, and then the three looked at Orion. He looked from face to face and attempted a partial Earth smile.

"I'll remember your offer," Brandon said. "We live in the country so we should be fine until he leaves.

Brandon, Audrina, and Orion began their trek back to their place in the country. The visit with the professor was very enlightening. Brandon mulled over in his mind that there is a civilization, in Orion, that not only is into exploring space; they *build* astronauts as well as equipment to do the same. Perhaps it's the only way to actually be successful at the endeavor. Space is a very harsh environment.

They left the city behind. Their destination was twenty-two miles into the country, this time, approaching from the south.

Suddenly, the back seat of the car was filled with a flash of a pinkish light. Orion became visible. Brandon quickly pulled over to the side of the road and stopped. Brandon and Audrina turned toward the back seat and stared at the belt around Orion's waist. Brandon looked up at the traffic passing by the car. "Orion, get down below window level."

Orion slid off the seat into the floor then looked up at Brandon and Audrina. *"There's someone else, close!"*

"Are they here to pick you up," Audrina asked.

"No!" Orion said. *"It's another member of our team!"*

"Oh my God," Brandon exclaimed, "another survivor?"

Orion removed the second Initiator from his belt and handed it to Audrina then keyed his cloaking function and became invisible again.

"Orion," Audrina said, "did that flash make you visible?"

"No, I did it. You can't remove the Initiator while cloaked."

Audrina, sphere in hand, turned toward Brandon: "We know the routine." She opened her purse, took out a note pad, then checked and logged the time. Brandon steered the car back onto the road and proceeded to the next exit a quarter of a mile ahead. He pulled off onto a blacktop road, drove 500 yards, made a U-turn, then pulled over and parked to wait for the next flash.

GMO Testing Area—Houston

EBE sat in the sunroom in a small chair slowly rubbing what was left of his right arm. It gets too warm when he's in the Sun's rays. If he ever gets home, he will get a new arm. He looked up at the Sun, then back down and through the small viewing port at the highway far in the distance across the fields of greenery. He could barely see the cars going by in both directions, going where they want to go. Without warning, the Locator function of his belt flashed a pinkish light. His eyes snapped to it.

"They are here, finally, they're here!" He jumped to his feet and walked back and forth rubbing his damaged arm and waiting for the next flash that would tell him how far away they were. If they did not arrive before his sunroom time was up, he would have to conceal the Locator port to hide

the flashes. Just over an hour later, the unit flashed again. The distance formulated in his mind in seconds. He converted it to Earth measure. Thirty-four miles….

Chapter 13

THE HUNT

Roswell—Monday morning, 7:00 a.m.

Agent Stockton, standing before the mirror, splashed his face with Afta Pre Shave Lotion then plugged in his razor. When he looked at his image, he froze for a moment. His mind formed a picture of EBE looking up at him and asking about his own kind coming for him. The thought grew in intensity. The image of the alien was superimposed over his image in the mirror. Stockton gritted his teeth suppressing an urge to scream then laid his hand on the mirror. The image of EBE dissolved leaving Stockton's tense face. The agent paused a moment, took a couple of deep breaths, then began shaving.

The UFO museum opened at 9:00 a.m. He and Wilson would make that their first stop, ask a few prudent questions, and then proceed to visit all the crash sites. It wasn't likely that the first day's work would yield anything but it was the logical first step.

The two agents went to Denny's, entered the restaurant and were escorted to a table. Gertie

Wells, seated at the cash register, spotted them as soon as they entered the door. She watched them follow the receptionist across the room to be seated. She studied the two men for a few moments. The young one was sharply dressed. He tied a double Windsor in his tie. Handsome. Gertie picked up the phone.

Elizabeth Rainwater, just arriving, sat down behind her desk to review the day's schedule. Three appointments—follow-ups. The phone rang. She picked it up.

"Liz?" came from the receiver.

"Hello, Gertie."

"They're here." Elizabeth leaned back in her chair. Gertie continued: "A white man, 45ish and a young black guy about 25. They might as well have signs on their backs. The young one is cute."

"Gertie—shame," Elizabeth said and chuckled. "I think I'll take a few days off; besides there's something I'd like to do."

Elizabeth hung up the phone then picked it back up and made another call. "Have doctor Walton take all my appointments for a few days. I want to take care of some personal business." She called the airport and booked an afternoon flight to Houston.

On her way out of the hospital to go home and pack a bag, she stopped at the vending machines, inserted a dollar, then reached down and picked up a bag of M&Ms and dropped it in her purse.

Rural Houston

Brandon, looking around the area, turned to Audrina, "We don't have a related checkpoint here. He could be anywhere."

Audrina nodded. "Let's find out how far away he is by measuring the time between the flashes then go home and scribe a circle on a county map. He'll be somewhere on that circle. We can pick likely places and begin the search."

"That's a good idea," Brandon joined. "If we get Orion within about 500 yards he'll sense him and can lead up to him."

"He can talk to him," Audrina added.

Houston

Sixty-eight minutes following the initial flash, the sphere repeated its function.

"Thirty-four miles," Audrina said. "Could be in any direction. He's somewhere on a 68 miles wide ring around us. We are now right in the middle.

Brandon pulled the car's gear selector into Drive then eased to the highway and looked at the signs on the intersection. Highway 6 and FM 1421.

Audrina made a note, then they headed for the Harris County Chamber of Commerce and then home.

When they got home and walked into the living room the phone was ringing. Audrina hurried over and picked it up. "Hello."

"Audrina, this is Elizabeth. They are here. Apparently they did pick up Orion's message."

"They came to see you?"

"Not yet. Gertie, a special friend, saw them at Denny's and called me. I decided to take a few days off, accept your invitation, and come to Houston for a visit. My plane arrives at 4:15."

"Wonderful," Audrina said. "We'll pick you up."

Brandon looked at his watch: 1:15 p.m. "Okay," he said. "We are going to have to leave at about 2:15 to get to the airport and into the building to the terminal on time. We've got an hour; let's work with this county map." He laid it out on the dining room table then located the compass. Audrina did the math. Thirty-four miles was four and one-quarter inches. He set the compass and scribed the line with the metal point of the tool on the intersection. They began to study the circle and what lay on its path.

"Let's eliminate, for now, the parts of the circle that pass through neighborhoods, industrial areas and barren ground," Brandon said. Audrina nodded then began to carefully study the path of the 200-mile circumference of the scribed circle.

There was a power substation, a city maintenance yard, barren ground, a large water reservoir, and then more barren ground. Next, a US Government Postal Service Vehicle Maintenance Facility, a possibility, a US Army National Guard Depot, another possibility. Brandon's pen continued to follow the scribed line; next, it passed over an Agricultural Testing Station. Definitely worth a look.

Brandon looked at his watch. They left Orion at home and headed for the airport to pick up a friend.

Roswell

Stockton and Wilson finished breakfast then handed Gertie their breakfast tab and a credit card. Gertie processed their ticket then gave the young Wilson a bright red lipstick smile. He returned the smile, and then he and his colleague headed for the UFO Museum.

There were a dozen people standing around in front of it waiting for the 9:00 a.m. opening. Momentarily an older man unlocked the door and held it open for the gathering crowd to enter. A staff member was waiting at the first exhibit to begin the first tour of the day. Stockton, entering the museum, stopped and stood by the staff member until the crowd was all inside. "How long have you been with the museum?" The attendant released the door and turned to the agent.

"Since we organized in '91; we got it ready, and opened it to the public in 1992."

"Anything significant happen since you've been open?"

"Well, the thing most exciting for us was the discovery that a second saucer crashed in the Lincoln National Forest in '47. That fact came to light in 1995. The Ragsdale Story. We have a book and a video about it in the gift shop."

"Nothing new lately?"

"Lots of people from all over, all over the world."

Stockton nodded and smiled then joined the gathering crowd for the impending tour of the museum.

Stockton, driving west of Old Pine Lodge Road, looked over at Wilson. "I think we should go ahead and take a look at the three sites; however, we are going to have to take a hard look at a conspirator."

"I agree," Wilson said. "If the *Creature* is actually here he would obviously have to have help; food, lodging. And why did he wait fifty years to send a message home?"

"Maybe he was on assignment to gather information and it took him that long to complete his task."

"Right under our noses?"

"Apparently."

Back at the motel, Stockton parked the car and they entered their room. "Our Missing Midget; who would likely help him?" Stockton said thoughtfully.

Wilson sat down at the room's round table and loosened his tie. "Religious types; nuns will help anybody, the elderly, doctors or nurses would be likely; our Missing Midget *was* in a crash, you know."

Stockton glanced at Wilson and nodded. "Let's find out who the doctors and nurses were that got involved when the crash occurred. It seems the most logical place to begin. However, they would be around eighty years old now. If we come up empty, we can start interviewing Roswell's Ministers."

Stockton picked up the phone and made the call. Minutes later, he had a list of four doctors and two nurses that were present at the fabled hangar in July 1947. He studied it for a moment.

"Okay," Stockton said, "tomorrow morning we start interviewing Roswell's medical people and see if we can establish a connection."

Houston

Brandon and Audrina drove into the George Bush Intercontinental Airport and parked the car. They made their way into the terminal to await Elizabeth's arrival. Sitting in the waiting area

Brandon laced his fingers together and began to surmise.

"We can start a systematic search tomorrow. It may take some time, but we'll find him. We have a proximity device locked onto him and Orion's built-in senses, we can't miss. I'm nervous about what circumstances we might find. It's not likely that there's another Elizabeth Rainwater taking care of him, hiding him, waiting for his rescue. I'm really afraid it might be more sinister."

Audrina glanced at the arrival gate then to Brandon. "There's no military base on or in the circle."

"There's a National Guard Depot."

"I suppose it could be used as a cover for…" Elizabeth came through the arrival gate. Brandon and Audrina stood; Audrina raised her arm and got Elizabeth's attention then met her and hugged her.

"Orion?" Elizabeth asked.

"He's at home."

"I have something for him," Elizabeth said then opened her purse and picked up the bag of M&M's.

Brandon's eyes went from the bag of candy to Elizabeth's face. "You're kidding."

"No," Elizabeth said. "He loves them. I think he likes that they are shaped like his ship." They laughed and started for the parking lot.

Brandon, pulling out of the parking lot and entering the traffic, glanced at Elizabeth. "We met Gertie when we were in Roswell, she's wonderful. Does she know about Orion?"

"Yes. She's a special friend, a true best friend. When I was seventeen, I started going to the Desert Cactus there in Roswell. It's where all the soldier boys went every Saturday night. I met Gertie there; she was twenty-one. We hit it off and became friends. It wasn't long until I knew she was a best friend. It's turned out to be a friendship that's lasted a lifetime. I introduced her to Orion in '53. Gertie is an M&M lover. When she came over for one of her visits she had a bag with her and offered Orion one. He tasted it and liked it. He became an M&M lover, too. I brought him some home from time to time."

Brandon and Audrina filled Elizabeth in on the Initiator signaling another survivor of the crash in Roswell and his presence here in the Houston area. Elizabeth was apprised of their quest to locate and possibly rescue the second member of Orion's team.

Elizabeth gravely offered an assessment: "He's most likely a captive by the CIA. The CIA was organized soon after the crash in Roswell. Orion's living situation was unique. My father was at the right place at the right time and was a compassionate man. This second alien that you are talking about was, more than likely, not so fortunate."

The fact that two agents were now in Roswell trying to find Orion was evidence that Elizabeth was right and the rescue, if possible, was not going to be easy. She feared for Orion. If something terrible went wrong, there would be two captives; Orion and his buddy. Orion could continue to be hidden and, maybe, never be found. However, he was on Earth; not his home. Being the only one of his kind wasn't a life. It was a challenge to survive, rescue his kind, and then get home. A quest worth the risk, however serious that might be.

Orion had projected to all: *"Get me close and I will go and get him."*

Orion sensed Elizabeth's presence as they turned off the Farm to Market road onto the long driveway to Brandon's and Audrina's property. He spoke: Elizabeth responded: "Well, Hello."

"Are you Okay?"

"Yes, I understand you have a friend here."

"Yes, we are going to find him."

"I'm glad. I have a gift for you...."

Chapter 14

CONTACT

Tuesday morning Brandon opened his closet door, reached up on the shelf above the clothes rack and picked up his pair of binoculars, and then he, Audrina, Elizabeth, and Orion, with the Initiator, drove back to the point of contact Monday afternoon.   As they neared the intersection, a new situation became evident. The proximity function of the sphere did not initiate. Audrina shook it, watching it intently. It remained dark.

"Either he's been moved or something is blocking the signal," Brandon said.

The group was quiet for a few minutes then Audrina broke the silence: "Let's start on our planned route and see if we can get lucky and get Orion close enough to sense something."

Brandon pulled the car into gear and began the drive to the first area of interest. The National Guard Depot; the closest objective.

As Brandon cruised by the small sign with a directional arrow—*National Guard Amory*—and continued on slowly.

"Orion, anything?"

"No, he's not here."

Brandon pulled over, reached for the map, and began plotting their course to the next objective. Suddenly, the sphere in Audrina's hand flashed.

GMO Testing Area—26 Miles Away

EBE stepped through the adjoining door from the tool room into the sunroom, holding his left hand over the Locator port on his waist-worn device. He saw the flash between his fingers. Fortunately, the guard took no notice. EBE had managed to conceal it. He waited for the next flash and the information that would come with it. How much closer are they? He peered through the viewing port again.

Audrina quickly opened her purse, picked up her pad and pen and made a note of the time. The wait for the next flash began. They sat quietly, marking time; each minute seeming like an eternity. Minutes later, in the quiet, a crunching sound followed by rhythmic faint chewing sounds came from the seemingly empty back seat behind Brandon. They all looked at each other and then settled back into the wait.

At minute number fifty-two the anticipated flash occurred.

"Okay!" Brandon said, and then grabbed the Road Atlas. "Twenty-six miles." He noted the terrain and businesses on the scribed line. Behind them was barren ground, the water reservoir, and suburbia. Ahead was a housing addition, open ground, and then the Agricultural Testing Area some twenty-five or twenty-six miles ahead.

"That's got to be it!" Brandon exclaimed. He postured himself behind the wheel and began traversing the distance taking the best routes available. The flashes of the sphere grew closer and closer together.

"Why didn't it flash when we first got to this area? We were within range." Audrina said.

"If he was underground it would block the signal," Orion projected.

"Then they brought him up top for some reason," Brandon added.

"Sunlight. We need sunlight," Orion included.

Audrina turned and looked at Elizabeth sitting behind her. "You think we might actually get lucky here?"

Elizabeth answered, "They may have settled into a routine here that's been in place for years; perhaps developing a relaxed posture, and that may work to our advantage. Orion can walk right in, when invisible, if the door's open. He could simply get close to his friend and they would both be invisible. When I was twelve, I used to disappear with Orion for fun. Mom and Dad made me stop. They were afraid I might get hurt and they wouldn't know it."

Brandon, with the sphere flashing every fourteen seconds, approached the GMO TESTING AREA. Suddenly, Orion became visible, crouched down in the seat, and was completely still for several moments. He looked up at his three companions.

"EBE, it's EBE!" he projected. Orion was quiet and still for several minutes.

"He's still alive?!" Brandon exclaimed.

Audrina, staring at Orion, offered: "They must have faked his death to ward off everybody digging into the rumors about him."

"Years and years here?" Elizabeth muttered, "That's awful."

"He's in a sunroom on the surface," Orion declared. *"I'm going in and get him."*

"Orion," Audrina said, "you're visible." Orion promptly disappeared.

All eyes went to the research facility out in the field. "My, God," Brandon said. "Look at that fence. It's at least ten feet high and there's barbed wire around the top."

Orion projected to EBE: *"Can we get in?"* The answer from EBE was instant.

"The code is 19016."

Roswell

Agent's Stockton and Wilson stood before the information bulletin board in the lobby of the Loveless Regional Hospital.

138

"Okay," Stockton said, "we've eliminated the two military doctors, and a doctor Camden, deceased, no heirs. That leaves this one. Dr. Elizabeth Rainwater. Her father, Compton C. worked on the aliens in '47. It might be a long shot but I want to talk to her." Wilson looked at the names list.

"She's down the hall." He said, pointing.

Stockton stuck his head in Elizabeth's office door. Empty. He stepped to the next office. "Is next door the right office for Dr. Rainwater?"

"She's on vacation; left yesterday."

"When's she due back?"

"Don't know, Sir. She said a few days; personal business. May I help you; I'm taking her appointments?"

"No, thank you. I'll check back later,"

Walking back down the hall toward the exit, Agent Wilson glanced at Stockton. "Dr. Compton Rainwater was involved with the aliens in '47. One of the aliens managed to elude capture, holed up somewhere, and then, a few days ago, it sent a message home. Azell picked it up and reported to you that the message from the Missing Midget had been sent and that it came from Roswell. We were dispatched to come here and find this alien. We were intercepted and taken to Houston to meet EBE, another of the aliens. EBE read your mind and asked if his people had arrived. We were brought back here to engage in the hunt and find the one that sent the message."

Agent Stockton stopped in the hallway and focused on Wilson's face. Wilson continued: "We checked out the area, and then focused on a conspirator believing that someone must have helped the Missing Midget. We eliminated all possibilities down to one doctor, more specifically, his daughter, who is also a doctor. We go to see her. Guess what? She's out of town." Then Wilson paused and took a deep breath. "Agent Charles Manly Stockton, our Dr. Elizabeth Rainwater is in Houston."

Stockton stared at Wilson's face for a long moment then looked at the floor then back to his face. "No wonder they call you the budding young genius. Where in Houston?"

"I don't know," Wilson said, "but I'll bet you money that she shows up at EBE's address."

Stockton paused a moment in thought. "I've got a gut feeling that you are right, however, before we go screaming to Houston or even make a telling phone call, let's search Elizabeth Rainwater's house. If she harbored our Missing Midget there for half a century there will be something; something to let us know for sure."

"Agreed."

Stockton stepped over to the information desk on the way out of the hospital.

"Do you have a phone book?" Stockton made a note of an address.

The agents entered the Post Office, got in line and waited. Soon they were directed to Jim in the corner and they asked directions to Route 3, Box 121.

"Lots of people looking for Dr. Rainwater," Jim said then explained directions out on Old Pine Lodge Road.

"Lots of people?" Wilson inquired.

"Yeah, last week a young couple came in here and asked who lived at Box 121."

"Who were they:"

"Don't know. I never seen them before. I can tell you what it is. There's talk around town that that old house is haunted.

"Really?"

"People claim they've seen ghosts out there; weird looking creatures, that just disappear." Stockton and Wilson looked at each other, thanked Jim, and went to their car.

Rural Houston

"Are you sure?" Brandon said, "Something might go wrong and you will be a captive also."

"I have to go. I can't leave him there."

"But what about the guard?" Audrina said. "There's going to be a guard."

"Elizabeth's probably right," Brandon said. "They, no doubt, have brought him up for his daily sunshine a thousand times and consider it routine. However, when they discover that he's gone, all hell will break loose."

"I have communicated to EBE my plan to rescue him. I have the entrance code for the gate. I'm going to go in cloaked and then go to the complex and locate his sunroom. Then I will project to the guard that he wants a cup of coffee, gently, over and over. When he goes. I'll unlock EBE's door, bring him into my cloaking field, and we will simply walk out." Orion extended his hand toward Audrina. *"Let me have his Initiator. I will insert it into his Locator Device as soon as I find him; just in case we get caught."*

Orion inserted EBE's Initiator into the slot of his belt and prepared to go. *"I'll get out of the car here. You can't be this close if an alarm goes off or something. Go ahead and drive down to the next intersection make a turn then stop. We will come to you."*

Orion, I don't like this," Brandon said.

"I can do it."

"Okay," Brandon said reluctantly, "we'll be waiting; good luck."

Brandon opened the back door and Orion stepped out.

Chapter 15

THE OASIS

Agent Stockton turned off Old Pine Lodge Road onto the winding dirt road leading to a grove of trees a mile and a half into the desert. Minutes later, he pulled up into the yard of the older two-story house and killed the engine. Wilson reached inside his suit coat pocket, retrieved a pair of thin buckskin gloves, and put them on. Stockton did the same.

"Let's knock on the door just to be sure."

"There's nobody home, trust me," Wilson answered.

"Still..."

Wilson gestured toward the door, followed Stockton up onto the porch, and waited for his verification. Silence. Stockton tried the door. It was open. The agents entered the living room and looked around. They began opening drawers, and cabinets, careful to leave it like it was found; a slow tedious process.

Toward the back of the house, they entered the master bedroom and began systematically going through the chest and dresser. On the dresser top, there were pictures of Compton Rainwater and family. He, his wife and 1 child; Elizabeth. Opening the second drawer of the chest, agent Wilson picked up a leather bound picture album. He began leafing through it, looking at the pictures. He came to a full-page 8 x 10 photograph of a birthday party. A calendar hanging on the wall behind the birthday girl read: 1948. He counted thirteen candles. He froze.

"Stockton...come here."

Agent Stockton closed the dresser drawer, stepped over to Wilson side, and viewed the photo album. He was looking at a picture taken of a birthday party. A young girl was blowing out candles on a rectangle shaped birthday cake. A middle-aged woman was standing at her elbow. Wilson pointed a gloved finger at the lower left corner of the photograph.

There was a gray three-fingered hand resting on the table, visible from just above the wrist down.

"Okay," Stockton said and pulled his weapon, "let's take a look upstairs."

Wilson glanced at Stockton holding his gun. "You won't need that. He's in Houston. I'm telling you, man, he's in Houston."

"Just the same, let's check." Wilson complied and pulled his weapon as well and they headed up the wide stairway to the second floor. There was a door open on the left a few feet away from the head of the stairs. Stockton approached it and cautiously looked inside the room.

"Come here and look at this." Wilson followed Stockton into the room. Stockton continued: "A small bedroom, one twin size bed, a small antique dresser and chest, and then a 50-inch projection TV." Stockton holstered his weapon and began opening dresser drawers. When he got to the fourth drawer down, the bottom one, he pulled it open. It was completely full of empty M&M bags.

"You gotta' be kidding," Wilson breathed.

Chapter 16

RESCUE

GMO Testing Area - Houston

"Orion watched Brandon drive away and head for the concealment of the trees at the next intersection on the Farm to Market road. Then he began his trek down the blacktop road the four hundred yards to the gate of the testing station and EBE's prison. EBE sensed his proximity and was careful to keep the port on his belt covered.

Brandon, standing beside the car resting his elbows on its roof, binoculars in hand, focused them on the gate of the testing station. He saw the entrance pedestal with its keypad disappear for a moment, and then wink back on and the gate slowly lumbering down its track. It immediately returned to the closed position.

"He's inside," he announced. Elizabeth and Audrina were watching the testing station from a quarter mile away. Brandon reached down to the inside of the driver's door and pressed the trunk release. The trunk of the car rose to full open.

Orion entered the gate, then turned to the right and made his way down a dirt road the 500 yards to the equipment shed and office complex. The tool shed, sunroom, and offices were next to each other, constructed in a line. Behind was a four-foot tall crop of very green corn stalks waving in a gentle breeze. Orion sensed a guard sitting on a bench inside the tool shed. He was reading a Golf Digest magazine.

Orion began his projected suggestion. A few minutes later, the guard wet his lips with his tongue and turned another page on his magazine. As the minutes slowly passed, he began flipping the pages one after the other, glancing briefly at each page. Abruptly, he got up, stepped over to the sunroom entrance, closed a heavy dead bolt on the door, and then opened the outer door of the tool shed and walked over to the adjacent offices and entered. Inside he poured himself a cup of coffee then struck up a conversation with a lady sitting at her desk making computer entries.

Orion quickly entered the tool room, reached up, slid the dead bolt back out of the hasp, and pulled the door open. EBE stepped through the doorway and disappeared. Orion quickly inserted the Initiator into EBE's Locator Device. It immediately began a ten-second transmission, and then went dark. The two hurriedly began the trek back the quarter mile to the entrance gate.

Lagrange Point between Earth and its Moon

The Transfer Ship, upon reaching the Lagrange Point 195,505 from Earth, held and launched two Shuttles, one to Houston and one to Roswell. The rescue crafts would proceed to the original coordinates, then, if needed, transmit a request for an update.

GMO Testing Area - Houston

Bandon, watching through his binoculars, saw the large gate lumber open then close again. "They just came out of the gate!"

Audrina and Elizabeth strained to see the invisible. Then they and Brandon's minds were filled with Orion's words. *"We are out and on our way to you. EBE's coordinates have been transmitted. His rescue ship will come to Houston first, then update on his location. Mine will come to Roswell first, then update on my location."*

"Are they close?" Audrina asked.

"I don't know."

Silence fell on the car. The waiting was excruciating. Moments later, Elizabeth opened the passenger side, rear door and pushed it all the way open, then moved across the seat to the driver's side.

Finally, after what seemed like an eternity, they felt the gentle movement of the car and then the back door closed. Elizabeth couldn't help it; she reached into the generated field and felt of two bald heads. She leaned in, disappearing from the waist up, and hugged them both. It was EBE's first.

Brandon quickly closed the trunk, started the car and drove away.

The guard, draining his third cup of coffee, glanced at his watch. EBE's sunroom time was up ten minutes earlier. "I gotta' go," he said to the clerk, set his coffee cup on the sink, and headed for the tool shed. Stepping in the door, he saw the sunroom door standing open.

"They came up and got him," he muttered, "Scanlon's not going to like this." He reached over, opened the panel, and activated the elevator. When it opened into the lab below ground, he stepped out. All personnel were business as usual. He decided to leave well enough alone and went back to his station.

Roswell

Agent Stockton steered the car back onto Old Pine Lodge Road then drove back to the city.

"One more thing," Stockton said, "let's check the airport and see if Dr. Rainwater indeed flew to Houston."

Wilson looked over at Stockton; "How would you take an alien on an airplane?"

"Beats me. At this point, nothing would surprise me."

The line supervisor at the Roswell Airport looked at Stockton's ID then turned and brought up the records. "Yes, Dr. Elizabeth Rainwater flew to Houston on our Flight 417 yesterday afternoon."

"Was anybody with her?"

"No, Sir, she was alone."

Stockton paused a moment then: "Did she happen to have an unusually large piece of luggage with her?"

The supervisor frowned and checked the records again. "I show nothing unusual, Sir."

"Thank you," Stockton said then booked two tickets to Houston on the afternoon flight. They headed back to their motel room to check out. When Stockton unlocked the door and stepped in, he saw a red light on the desk phone blinking. He stepped over and picked up the receiver. The appliance buzzed the front desk. The clerk's voice came on the line.

"Mr. Stockton, there's a call waiting for you; I'll do the call back."

Azell's voice came on the line. "His people must be on their way. I received another message. It just said, *"Come and get me?'* It also gave coordinates."

"Where?"

"About thirty miles southwest of Houston."

Stockton almost dropped the phone. He hung it up and turned to Wilson.

"That was Azell. Our Missing Midget just sent another message—from thirty miles southwest of Houston."

"That's where the GMO Research Station is."

"Yeah."

Stockton and Wilson headed for the lobby to check out then to the airport.

Chapter 17

DANA CARAY

The Entomologist

Brandon drove up into the driveway of Professor Dana Caray. He stepped out of the car and rang the doorbell. The professor answered the door himself.

"Well, hello, you dropping off your alien?" he said then smiled broadly.

"Professor, I have someone who wants to say hello. Is your Caregiver here now?"

"No, she's grocery shopping."

Brandon motioned to Audrina. She, Elizabeth, and two cloaked residents of the Alnilam Solar System got out of the car and filed up the walk. Professor Caray stepped back and swung the door full open. The parade entered and he closed it.

"Orion," Brandon said.

Orion and EBE became visible. EBE projected: "Hello, Professor Dana."

"Oh My God, EBE!" The professor spontaneously hugged him, and then noticed his missing right limb. "What happened to your arm!?" EBE explained his attempt to escape and the trap that stopped him. "Orion came for me and this time we made it." Dana Caray turned to Orion and smiled. "Way to go, Orion."

Orion again tried his, work in progress, Earth smile.

Alice, Professor Dana Caray's Caregiver and live-in maid, drove up the driveway from the grocery store and parked beside Brandon's car. She got out, picked up two bags of groceries and entered the front door. Professor Caray pointed at EBE and Orion then to the doorway to the next room. They quickly stepped around the door out of sight. Alice walked into the dining room and put the two bags on the table then stepped into the open doors of the professor's study. She nodded at his guest.

"Alice," professor Caray began, "you remember Mr. Stevens and his wife."

"Of course,"

Professor Caray indicated Elizabeth. "This is a friend of theirs, Dr. Elizabeth Rainwater." Alice nodded and smiled. The professor resumed: "Alice, I want you to brace yourself."

"Sir?"

"I want to introduce you to two more friends of theirs and mine. They are different."

"Different?"

"From another planet." Alice laughed glancing from face to face.

"Funny, Professor, very funny."

Professor Caray said: "Orion, EBE." They stepped around the door in view of Alice. Alice

154

stared for several moments then looked from face to face again.

"This is Orion and this is EBE. They are from the Alnilam Solar System in the Orion Constellation." Alice nodded toward the two.

"Are you okay?" Elizabeth asked.

Alice's eyes went to Elizabeth's face. "I think so." Alice paused a moment then: "This is real, isn't it?"

"Do you remember the Roswell Incident of 1947?" Brandon asked.

"Yes, I saw the movie."

"These guys were on those ships," Audrina said.

Alice's caregiver's heart spoke: "What happened to your arm?" EBE projected the response. Alice touched her head, took a couple of deep breaths then relaxed and smiled. "This is cool."

Elizabeth and Alice, cut from the same cloth, began talking, then went out together to get the rest of the groceries out of her car.

Professor Caray looked at Brandon. "Good, no heart attack."

Brandon laughed.

Professor Caray addressed the group: "Could we have an early dinner here and make an afternoon of it—just visit for a while? These guys, Orion and EBE, are going to be leaving and we will never see them again in our lifetimes."

"Girls," Alice said, "let's prepare a nice meal while these guys talk shop." She looked at Orion and EBE: "you are guys; right?" They both nodded. Alice smiled

"Talk shop?" Orion projected.

Brandon smiled. "Discuss what we are going to do next."

"Oh."

"Professor," Brandon began, "their people are on their way and will probably be here soon. They've received two different distress transmissions. Question; where should we take EBE and Orion for pickup?"

Professor Caray didn't hesitate. "Roswell; it's where it all started. It's only fitting that it end's there."

Brandon nodded then he and the professor looked at Orion and EBE. Orion was examining EBE's damaged arm, holding it with both his hands and the long slender fingers. Orion sensed them and looked around.

"He'll be getting a new one."

"You can do that?!" the professor exclaimed.

Orion and EBE both nodded.

The girls called dinner.

Chapter 18

EMPTY PRISON

Stockton and Wilson sat in the airport waiting to board. Stockton stepped over to a public phone station, pick it up, and dialed, gave his calling code numbers, then waited for an answer. Elliot Scanlon, regional director for the CIA answered.

Stockton spoke guardedly, "Our Missing Midget is in Houston."

"What!?" Scanlon exclaimed. "How do you know?"

"Azell picked up another transmission. It came from thirty miles southwest of Houston."

"Oh My God! That's right on top of us."

"We are boarding a flight there in a few minutes."

"As soon as you land, get out here to the facility. I'm locking it down."

"Yes sir."

Scanlon ordered the GMO TESTING AREA locked down. He ordered four guards on the outer gate. Nobody in, nobody out. He picked up his office phone and called down in the hole. Security answered.

"Double the guard on EBE." Scanlon said.

"Sir, he's not down here; he's still up in the sunroom."

Scanlon looked at his watch, slammed down the phone, jumped up, ran out of the offices to the tool shed, and jerked the door open. The adjoining door to the sunroom still stood wide open.

"Oh my God!" he screamed and ran out into the middle of the road by the high security fence and looked around in all directions. Nothing. He swore, rushed back into the elevator and pushed the button to descend into the holding area. When the elevator arrived and the door opened the full contingency of security were gathered for instructions.

"EBE's not up there. Search all the offices, now, quickly." Security hurriedly combed the under-ground office complex. Nothing.

"Who took him up today?"

One of the guards, a caged look on his face, stepped forward. "I did."

"Did you bring him back down?"

"No, I locked him in the sunroom and stepped over to the offices and got some coffee. When I came back, the door to the sunroom was open. I thought that someone from down here came up and got him."

Scanlon swore again then ordered everyone up top immediately.

"The testing station is completely locked down. I want every square foot of this farm searched, every row of corn, every piece of equipment, every building, every shed, everything. We can't lose him. Go!!!"

158

Chapter 19

HOMEWARD BOUND

"Let's take my RV," Professor Caray said, "I could use one more adventure."

Brandon pushed his plate back and looked around the table. "We should go to Roswell right away. Since they have signaled already, they may show at any time."

"Audrina offered: "We can stock the RV kitchen with coffee, and snacks."

Professor Caray went into his study, opened the top drawer of his desk, picked up the key to his RV and handed it to Brandon. "Go pull it around front and let's get this adventure of a lifetime going. Leave it running."

Brandon complied then came back into the house. Alice, Audrina, and Elizabeth quickly stocked the galley of Professor Caray's RV, his favorite pastime since his retirement. Alice had considered her job a perpetual vacation. This one would take the cake.

Brandon steered the Recreational Vehicle onto Interstate 10 West, out of Houston, then set the cruise at a modest 60 mph. The Sun was approaching the horizon in front of them; low enough to come streaming through the windshield. Brandon glanced across the dash. The professor, in the right hand seat, pointed at a plastic tray containing several pairs of sunglasses. Brandon picked up a pair and put them on.

"Professor," he said, "you have a nice machine here."

"Yes. We've had this thing all over the country the past few years. I had quite a wish list and Alice threw in a couple of destinations."

Orion and EBE were glued to the tinted picture window over the table. As they watched the terrain go by, they occasionally pointed and communicated with each other. Brandon glanced at their reflection in the internal rear view mirror. He wondered at what speed they spoke to each other in their own language.

Brandon drove slowly along the dirt road then up into the yard of Dr. Elizabeth Rainwater's home. He and Professor Caray turned and looked at their *crew*, all napping. Audrina and Elizabeth were leaning back in their chairs. Orion and EBE had their heads resting on their arms on the dining table. There was a flickering of pink light from Orion's safety device. Brandon looked upward in the predawn sky. The Sun would be coming up momentarily. There was a bright *star* slowly descending toward the RV. Brandon stepped back to the table and shook Orion and EBE gently. They raised their heads. Audrina and Elizabeth looked up at Brandon. He spoke:

"They're here."

EBE and Orion hurried outside, stepped out into the open, and looked up at the glowing orb approaching high in the sky. It suddenly winked out; then, minutes later, it reappeared at treetop level then settled to the ground next to Professor Caray's RV. It was thirty feet in diameter. An oval section slowly opened and a ramp extended itself outward until it touched the ground in front of the ship. The group saw several occupants of Orion's and EBE's statue looking at the two refugees. They were backlighted with bright lights, enhancing the scene. Orion and EBE stepped onto the ramp. Three of the crewmembers from inside the rescue ship gathered around EBE and began examining his right arm. Brandon imagined that there must have been very many high-speed exchanges in their language.

He motioned to Orion, Orion stepped to the end of the ramp. "Orion," Brandon said, "didn't you say that there were two ships coming; one going to Houston for EBE and one to Roswell—this one—for you?"

"Yes, when the ship reaches Houston, it will signal for EBE."

"Can you radio that ship and give them a message?"

"Why?"

"Decoy," Brandon said. "You've watched thousands of Earth movies. Make the people at that prison think that that ship picked up you and EBE and left Earth with you."

Orion held Brandon's eyes for a moment, and then his smile got more practice. He stepped up the ramp and conversed with the ship's commander. The leader turned to the communications console. Seconds later, he nodded at Orion.

"Brandon," Orion projected, *"that ship is approaching the Houston area. It will cloak, fly into the GMO TESTING AREA, and land in the cornfield. Then it will de-cloak, glow very brightly, ascend fifty feet, then zoom away at a high rate of speed and continue until it's out of sight. It will then meet us at the Transfer Ship."*

Orion, standing on the end of the ramp, surveyed the Earthlings that had meant so much to him after falling victim to a deadly mishap some fifty years earlier. He sensed the sadness in each of them. Elizabeth had a tear on one cheek. Audrina had moist eyes. Professor Dana and Brandon had the countenance of one about to experience a personal loss. He had come to understand humans having spent fifty years studying their culture. They had a heart to help. A heart to help....

Orion held up one of his long fingers in a *one-moment* gesture, and then stepped into the ship. Moments later, he reappeared and handed Brandon and Audrina a duplicate of the Keepsake.

"Keep this; if my assignments allow me to come this way again, I'll be able to find you. I will remember you Brandon Stevens, Audrina

Stevens, Elizabeth Rainwater, Professor Dana Caray, and you too, Caregiver Alice."

Orion smiled his last Earth smile, walked up into the ship, and the ramp closed. The spherical ship took on a glow, slowly rose up above the treetops, paused, and then quickly disappeared into the early morning sky.

End

ABOUT THE AUTHOR

Dan Holt is a U.S. Army veteran, having served three years as a Communications Specialist in Germany. He spent the remainder of his civilian career as a self-taught engineer, designing and testing large-scale production equipment for the file folder industry. The efficiency and durability of his designs even garnered interest from some foreign manufacturers.

In retirement, Dan has used his writing skills to express his continuing fascination with machinery and science fiction. His zest for adventure and intrigue continue to rule in KEEPSAKE and his previous published works: UNDERNEATH THE MOON, UNDERNEATH THE MOON 2, and SLEEP MODE. With over 5,000 copies of Underneath The Moon sold in the first six months, and the first month sales of over 1,000 copies of Underneath The Moon 2, Dan is now beginning work on his third novel in the *Underneath the Moon Series.* You can see all of his books on his Publisher's page at: www.maxholtmedia.com.